PENGUIN CANADA

FRACTURES

Budge Wilson was born and educated in Nova
Scotia but spent many years in Ontario. She
now lives in a fishing village on the South
Shore, Nova Scotia. She has won many awards
for her writing, including the Canadian
Library Association's Young Adult Book
Award, the Ann Connor Brimer Award, the
City of Dartmouth Book Award, first prize for
fiction at the CBC Literary Competiton, and
many Canadian Children's Book Centre Our
Choice Awards. Her collection of short stories
The Leaving was named a Notable Book by
the American Library Association and was
later included on its list of "The 75 Best
Children's Books of the Last 25 Years."

FRACTURES

Family Stories by

Budge Wilson

PENGUIN CANADA

Published by the Penguin Group

Penguin Books, a division of Pearson Canada, 10 Alcorn Avenue, Toronto, Ontario,
Canada M4V 3B2

Penguin Books Ltd, 80 Strand, London WC2R ORL, England

Penguin Putnam Inc., 375 Hudson Street, New York, New York 10014, U.S.A.

Penguin Books Australia Ltd, 250 Camberwell Road, Camberwell, Victoria 3124, Australia

Penguin Books India (P) Ltd, 11, Community Centre, Panchsheel Park,
New Delhi – 110 017, India

Penguin Books (NZ) Ltd, cnr Rosedale and Airborne Roads, Albany, Auckland 1310,
New Zealand

Penguin Books (South Africa) (Pty) Ltd, 24 Sturdee Avenue, Rosebank 2196, South Africa

Penguin Books Ltd, Registered Offices: 80 Strand, London WC2R ORL, England

First published 2002

5 7 9 10 8 6 4

Copyright © Budge Wilson, 2002

"The Metaphor" and "Mr. Manuel Jenkins" are from *The Leaving* © 1991 by Budge
Wilson, reprinted with the permission of House of Anansi Press. "Dreams" from *Cordelia
Clark* © 1994 by Budge Wilson, reprinted with the permission of Stoddart Publishing.
"My War" by Budge Wilson from *Notes Across the Aisle* (Thistledown Press, 1995).
"Carlotta's Search" by Budge Wilson from *When I Went to the Library* (ed. Debora
Pearson, A Groundwood Book/Douglas & McIntyre, 2001).

All rights reserved. Without limiting the rights under copyright reserved above, no part
of this publication may be reproduced, stored in or introduced into a retrieval system,
or transmitted in any form or by any means (electronic, mechanical, photocopying,
recording or otherwise), without the prior written permission of both the copyright
owner and the above publisher of this book, or in the case of photocopying in Canada,
without a license from the Canadian Copyright Licensing Agency (CANCOPY).

*Publisher's note: This book is a work of fiction. Names, characters, places and incidents
either are the product of the author's imagination or are used fictitiously, and any
resemblance to actual persons living or dead, events, or locales is entirely coincidental.*

The author wishes to thank the Canada Council for assistance in the writing of this book.

Manufactured in Canada.

NATIONAL LIBRARY OF CANADA CATALOGUING IN PUBLICATION

Wilson, Budge
Fractures / Budge Wilson.

ISBN 0-14-331201-4

1. Family—Juvenile fiction. I. Title.

PS8595.I5813F34   2002   jC813'.54   C2002-901234-1
PZ7

Visit Penguin Books' website at **www.penguin.ca**

In memory of two fine mentors,
Freda Pipe and Professor Lindsay Bennet

Table of Contents

Introduction	ix
Like a Water Lily	1
Two Diaries	25
Fathers	43
Dreams	59
Confusion	69
Crybaby	83
Mr. Manuel Jenkins	97
My War	117
Brothers and Sisters	129
Carlotta's Search	143
Mothers	153
The Metaphor	171

Introduction

A fracture is not always a break. Usually it's a crack, and sometimes a small one. The families in these stories are often fractured—seldom entirely broken, but flawed on several levels. But to some degree I think that this is true of most families. Many of us have less than perfect memories of our childhood homes, and our own children will look back on the places we have created for them, and will recall many experiences that were not as wonderful as we would have liked them to be. But in many cases, a lot of those difficulties will eventually make us wiser and more sensitive people. At the very least, we will know that we are not alone.

The adolescents and teens in these stories are of many ages—some younger than you are, and some older. If they are older, you will probably be curious about what lies ahead for you. The stories about younger ones may make you do another kind of wondering. But I feel that reading and thinking about people younger than you are may help you to understand who you are now, because of a realization of who you used to be. You may think, "Hey! That reminds me of the years when I was so shy"; or "That's the way I used to feel about my sister"; or "The father in this story is a lot like mine"; or "I felt exactly like that, and I still do."

Teenagers know that life is not easy. But so do we who read and write about them. We're all in this together. That time of life tends to be very intense. It's a picture that's painted in primary colours—bright reds, yellows, blues. You don't see much grey or beige, but there's quite a lot of jet black. The fears and angers and sorrows that you feel are very dark.

Metaphor

But life will probably also hand you many deep pleasures and a lot of amazing surprises. We know this, too. For many of you, life can be a pretty astonishing and satisfying adventure.

I hope that the adults in your world will read this book, too, recalling who they once were and accepting who they have become—with more respect for their own imperfections and anxieties. As a result, they may look at their own children in a new way, or may see the events and perceptions of their own childhood with a sharper focus. The fears and confusions felt by adults, as well as the joys encountered, are not so radically different from those experienced by children and teens. Sometimes it can be useful for all of us to remember that fact.

Like a Water Lily

Lida Snider is the kind of kid who never gets picked first for teams. Any kind of team. It doesn't seem to matter which. Softball teams, dodge ball teams, spelling bees. Today the teacher says, "Okay, George, you be the leader for Team A. Helena, you be the leader for Team B. We're going to take turns choosing, like we always do. George, you start."

This time it's dodge ball. In dodge ball, one team stands in the middle of a circle, which is ringed with members of the opposite team. The teacher hands someone (George in this case) a basketball or soccer ball. Then the slaughter begins. Turning this way and that way, with crafty subterfuge and skill, he will try to hit a member of the other team with the ball. But below the knees, please. Sometimes, people get hit above the knees—in the stomach, the groin (boys doubled up with agony, guffaws from the other boys, titters from the girls), or the breast. (The girls are thirteen now, and most of them have breasts—half grapefruits or fried eggs. No matter which, they're sure that those blows will lead directly to breast cancer.) These attacks to the wrong parts of the body are assumed to be the result of either poor coordination or evil intentions. Depending on who is throwing the ball, judgments are made with regard to this issue.

Dodge ball is a lot of fun for those who have speed built into their muscles and a set of finely tuned reflexes. The balls come fast and they come hard. It doesn't matter how often the phys ed instructor says, "The point of this game is to strike your opponent, not to maim him"; there will always be people who are heavily into maiming. Such, alas, is the human race. Also, to be fair, it is not easy in this game to be speedy and gentle at the same time. When you get hit by the ball, you're out. Out of the circle. Out of the game. Gradually, the outer circle demolishes the other team. But it may take a long time. In the meantime, a lot of valuable cardiovascular exercise takes place.

The kids stand in a straggly line on one side of the gym. The confident ones look straight ahead. The others study the floor or their fingernails, reluctant to lay bare their fears or their longings. George calls "Mary!"; Helena shouts "Harry!" Then it's Tiffany, Joe, Jeanie, Jack, up and down the line, selecting the desirables, ignoring the others, until there is no choice but to pick up the dregs. Lida is the last to be chosen. She stands alone by the wall, eyes fixed on the floor, thumb and index finger rubbing each other—rubbing, rubbing. Helena says (no longer shouting), "Lida." She says it like a sigh. It's a flat, weary sound: "Lida."

"I always get stuck with Lida," says Helena to Harry, in a voice loud enough for Lida to hear. "Oh, well."

There is nothing inherently wrong with Lida's coordination. Or her speed, for that matter. She has it in her—hidden, disguised, mislaid, unrecognized—to be a crack dodge ball player. Why is it, then, that she's always picked last? The oversimplified answer is that the kids don't like her. And something happens to kids who always get picked last. It doesn't take long for them to believe that they're no good. Furthermore, people who think they're no good, move (or jump or spell or catch or dance or run) with less speed and accuracy and grace than they're basically capable of. Unless their spirits are very, very strong. Then the kid in question may perform with an excellence that is born of anger—the desire "to show the bastards what I can do." But Lida doesn't fit into this category. She's become clumsy in spite of her genes.

As the balls come whizzing across the floor at her, Lida feels both frightened and wilted. Fear can take you a long way in dodge ball, but feeling wilted is fatal. Lida's a prime target, and she gets it once in the stomach and twice in the breast before George whams her in the ankle. *Out.* Last chosen. First out. Not a shortcut to popularity. "Klutz!" growls Tiffany, a fairylike child with wide grey eyes and a tumble of blond curls. She's been told she's beautiful since the day she was born. She stands like a duchess. She moves like an angel. She's never picked last.

Phys ed is the final period of the day. Afterwards, there's play practice in the auditorium and gymnastics in the all-purpose room. Other kids disperse to swimming at the Y, piano lessons, or maybe to home and two hours of TV.

Lida walks home alone. She hopes her father and mother are out. She plans to go up to the bathroom and look at herself in the cracked full-length mirror. She wants to inspect herself for a long time and figure out what's wrong with her. Her father's out of a job right now, so he might be in the kitchen drinking beer, or in the living room, asleep over the soaps. Her mother only works in the mornings on Tuesdays (but full-time the rest of the week) at Wal-Mart, in the back of the store—sorting, piling, lifting—so she might be home, too. But if Lida's lucky, they'll be out. She doesn't want to hear her father's raspy snoring or her mother's whining. She wants to be alone.

The house is empty. Lida smiles a pleased tight smile. Everything about Lida is tight. But this probably won't show up in the mirror. Without stopping for the one arrowroot biscuit she's permitted after school, Lida goes straight upstairs to the bathroom and locks the door behind her. She puts her backpack on the toilet seat, places her jacket neatly on top, and turns around to face the mirror.

It's hard to get a perfect sense of what she really looks like. The crack in the mirror runs horizontally right through the middle, and as a result Lida's top half doesn't join up neatly with her bottom half. Never mind. This is the best she can hope for. She stands there and carefully inspects her crooked self for a long, long time.

She's dressed much like everyone else, so her clothes tell her nothing. Blue T-shirt, jeans, Nikes. The uniform of the day. Because she's so thin, she knows that her knees look knobbly in her gym suit, but so do Helena's, and she gets to be a team leader, time after time. So knobbly knees can't be it. No earrings. She'd like to have pierced ears, but her mother says that this can wait till her dad gets another job. "*Whenever that might be,*" she says in a high voice, so that her husband will be sure to hear. "We need food more than we need foolishness," she continues. (It costs money to get your ears pierced. Plus the earrings.) "Or liquor," her mother adds.

Lida knows that her father lost his last job because of drinking. You can't live in a small house with paper-thin walls without knowing every family secret in the book. Not if your mom and dad do a lot of yelling at each other, especially at night when they think you're asleep. As though anyone could sleep through that racket.

Having eliminated her knobbly knees and her clothes as reasons for her lack of social success, Lida decides to investigate her face. Her whole head, in fact. Her hair is probably all right. It's just brown, which isn't wonderful (she's thinking about Tiffany's bouncing blond curls), but on the other hand it's not terrible. It has a bit of a wave, and the cut is okay. It's not as though it's sticking out in spikes or lying limp with grease. It's just, well . . . *hair*. Face next. She smiles at herself, animated, eager. Undeniably good teeth, and a nose that is neither good nor bad. No pink cheeks here; but no pimples, either. Large green eyes with short, straight lashes. Indifferent eyebrows. A clear, high forehead. A nothing face. But the smile is captivating. Her eyes crinkle up, giving off sparks, and faint splotches of colour touch her sallow cheeks. Lida is delighted with herself. Anyone seeing that girl in the mirror would pick her first. And even with her midsection distorted in the cracked mirror, she can see that her posture is perky and proud. She turns this way and that, displaying her minuscule breasts, giving herself sly glances, lifting an arrogant chin, feeling like a model. "I'd like me if I was them," she whispers, and leaves the room.

The minute she turns her back on the mirror, her smile disappears. It melts away as though attacked by a flash chinook. She can sense the collapse of her face as the smile vanishes. Her cheeks are heavy, her eyes feel pulled down at the corners. Already she is depressed again. The model, the cover girl, is gone. Her shoulders, held so erect and firm just moments ago, slump forward. Her stomach is out, her chest is in. She's right back where she was before she entered the bathroom. She's the same old Lida. As she passes a high mirror in the hall, she accidentally sees herself as she really is: sullen, defeated, unchosen.

Supper that evening is not a success. Mr. Snider is ticking it off in the living room, and no one tries to wake him up. Lida's mother eats silently, and sighs a lot. Being married to an alcoholic and working in the stockroom of Wal-Mart is not what she wants out of life. Besides, the store is way over on the other side of Dartmouth. It takes a long time to get there, a long time to get back to Halifax. And dragging all those groceries home on the bus on her only free afternoon isn't exactly a holiday. She's tired.

Mrs. Snider loves Lida and even thinks she's rather pretty. All that perfect skin. When she was that age, she had acne. Also, Lida gets good grades and helps with the housework. She should be proud of her. Perhaps she is. If so, she's not telling anyone. Lida's presence, her existence, isn't enough to compensate for Mrs. Snider's boredom, her sense of injustice, her certainty that God, or whoever else is in charge, has handed her a bag full of lemons. Today she's feeling particularly angry at life, and she's wishing that her daughter didn't choose to look so beaten down all the time.

"For heaven's sake, Lida," she says, "sit up straight. You look like a rag doll. And not the kind that anyone would want to hug."

Lida looks at the canned peas and the fried bologna on her plate, and knows that she's never going to get through this meal. At least there's a baked potato. She slathers it with margarine and picks away at it.

Mrs. Snider is off and running. "I had a rag doll when I was a kid. Made by my mother out of an old sheet, with yellow wool pigtails and an embroidered face. I loved that doll so much that I went to bed with her every night and took her everywhere I went. Finally, I hugged and kissed the face right off her. The embroidery strands just broke off and fell out, and first thing I knew I had a doll without a face."

Lida cheers up a bit. "So I guess you didn't like her anymore."

"Loved her as much as ever. My mom offered to embroider a new face on her, but I said no thanks. A new face wouldn't be *her*. I must have gone to bed with that faceless doll for another four years. For eight straight years, I hugged that doll."

A faceless doll, thinks Lida. The kind that anyone would want to hug. "What then?" she asks. "What happened to her?"

"The cloth material—the old sheet—got more and more rotten. Her stuffing kept leaking out, and long rips popped open in her arms and legs. Then one morning I woke up and found that I was holding a pile of feathers and fluff in my arms. Her whole belly had split from neck to groin. I guess I hugged that doll to death."

"Let's wake up Dad," suggests Lida. She loves her father, in spite of what his drinking is doing to all of them. Besides, she doesn't like where this conversation is going. She doesn't want to hear anything more about that huggable doll. Or her hug-crazed mother. She also takes dismal note of the fact that no one ever made *her* a rag doll. Lida can't remember the last time her mother hugged her. But from time to time her father does. And smooths her hair and says, "You're a good kid." Or sometimes, "I'm sorry."

"Let's wake him up," she says again.

Her mother says, "Let's not," and brings in the dessert. Two oatmeal cookies, one each. Store boughten. From the table, Lida can see her father sprawled on the living room sofa in his old stained blue sweatshirt and jeans. The sofa is covered with a flowered material, with roses, daisies, and tulips all over it. It's from the days, way back, when Mrs. Snider felt hopeful about a lot of things. She was going to have three yellow-haired children (she herself had been a blond)—two boys and, if she was still up to it, a chubby little girl. She'd have a pretty house with frilled sheer curtains and cheerful chintz on all her upholstered furniture. There'd be flowers in vases on every table. She'd keep her three Hummel figurines on the mantelpiece. They'd have a fire in the fireplace on rainy days and during blizzards. In Halifax, it's often chilly, even in summer. It's nice to sit beside a grate-fire and maybe toast marshmallows.

But the flowered sofa is as far as Mrs. Snider got. No fireplace, no mantel. Her Hummel figures live on top of her bureau in the bedroom, beside the box of Kleenex, among the tangle of lipsticks and loose earrings and pencils and grocery lists. No frilly curtains. Too expensive. Dark plaid flannelette drapes that double as curtains and blinds. Mrs. Snider sewed them by hand. She still had energy, back then, left over from the stockroom.

Lida is old enough now to wonder when her dad started drinking. Or did he always do it? Maybe he was able to hide it for a long time. It's easy for Lida to imagine feeling gloomy enough to want something to cheer you up, so maybe that's why he started. But he doesn't look very cheerful right now, splayed across the sofa and snoring into the faded pink satin cushion—a gift from a bridal shower fifteen years ago. And when he's awake and drinking, he doesn't act like it makes him feel better, either. At those times, he often gets mad at them and yells. He doesn't hit them or anything, but sometimes the things he says make Lida feel as though she's been hit. Like "Get that frown off your stupid face!" or "Are you too dumb to know when to shut up?" Stupid. Dumb. Later on, if he remembers anything about it, he says he's sorry. He tells her he didn't mean any of it. But he said it, didn't he? Why say something you don't mean, even if you're drunk? *Stupid face. Dumb.*

Lida's mother never says she's sorry. That's because she doesn't think she's done anything wrong. In fact, she thinks she's pretty wonderful. After all, doesn't she cook and clean, and work her butt off in the stockroom, and bring home the money that pays for the rent and the food and the beer? She doesn't know that she almost never smiles, that she tells her own stories but doesn't ask any questions. She never says, "How are things going, darling?" or "Was school fun today, sweetheart?" Never mind the darling and sweetheart bit. Those are words Lida's mother hasn't heard or used for over thirteen years. She's been growling and complaining ever since her husband came home from his first binge, swinging his beer bottles and calling her names. The ongoing combination of binges and growling has pretty well cut out the sweet talk on both sides. It was as though she forgot all those loving words even for Lida, whimpering in her playpen. Somewhere along the way, all the softness got sucked out of Mrs. Snider, and what rushed back in to fill up the empty space was rage. She doesn't really direct her wrath at Lida, but her anger is so black and blinding that she can't see beyond it to anything else. There's no sign attached to her chest saying, "It's not you I'm mad at."

Mrs. Snider, weary from lifting boxes and pushing carts, has fallen asleep watching TV. Lida washes up the supper dishes and goes upstairs to her room. If she had a sister, she could stop by her room and talk about all the things she's thinking. If the sister were older, she could ask her things. Find out what's wrong. If the sister were younger, Lida could maybe teach her stuff, show her how to be liked and chosen. Briefly, she thinks of her experience in the bathroom this afternoon. But she makes no deductions. In her mind, she calls the older sister Sally. She gives her younger sister a hug, and calls her Kitty.

The next day, Lida walks the four blocks to school, shoulders slouched over, eyes on the sidewalk. She can hear the groaner buoy moaning, way down in the harbour. She feels like that groaner buoy, making its awful *mmmmm-uh* sound, deep and tired. She feels like the fog that surrounds her—grey, heavy, slow-moving.

Maybe it's her name that's all wrong. Lida thinks of her non-sisters, Sally and Kitty, with their happy upbeat names. *Lida.* Pretty awful. Why would anyone stick a label like that on a tiny, innocent little baby? What on earth could her mother have been thinking of? *Lida.* What's worse: Lida Snider. "Lider Snider." She's heard kids call her that when she's done something unforgivable, like drop the ball at first base or miss the baton in a relay. Every time she hears it, she feels as though there's a peach pit in the centre of her heart—rough, hard.

As she continues on down Inglis Street, Lida comes abreast of the white house that's been for sale for the last two months. But not any more. Yesterday, she saw the moving van carting furniture into it—tables, chairs, a mattress, a birdcage, big and small cartons, a red bicycle, a piano. Lida didn't stay around long to watch. The house was big, and shiny with new paint. Also, it had a large veranda, with round, glossy spools supporting the railing. Lida wanted to live in that house and own that birdcage and the red bicycle. It made her miserable to be watching. Besides, she could see Tiffany coming along the street, trailing a gaggle of friends. Lida always feels uneasy when she's around Tiffany. She says nasty things about a lot of people, including Lida. Lida would like to take hold of all those blond curls and tear them out by the roots. But on that day, making a quick exit from the scene seemed the best move to make.

The front door of the white house opens, and a girl emerges. She's tall and has long, perfectly straight black hair. Even through the fog, Lida can recognize a quality in her that is strong, confident. The girl calls out to her, "Hey! Wait up!" and comes clattering down the front steps.

"Hi!" the girl says, stopping at the end of the front walk. She smiles, but somewhat shyly. So she's not an enemy. She's not standing there ready to pounce.

"Hi," says Lida, right back. And smiles. As always, when she smiles, her face is transformed, but it's a transformation that is seen by almost no one. A millionaire would pay a fortune to give his daughter those teeth. Although Lida's face is thin and oval, a dimple appears in each cheek.

"You going to Tower Road School?" says the stranger.

"Yes."

"Can I come with you? I think I know where it is, but I'm new. I could use some moral support."

"Sure," says Lida. She tells herself not to dare to hope. They'll tell her fast enough about Lider Snider.

"I'm Julie Halloway. What grade are you in? I'm in grade seven."

"Me, too." Julie. A cheerful name. She won't tell her she's Lida.

"Oh, good," says the stately Julie. "I hate starting new schools in the middle of the year. My dad's in the Navy. We move a lot. Last year, Victoria. Two years before that, Montreal. Now Halifax. I bet I'll just get to know some kids here, and we'll be off again. What's your name?"

"Lida." No way around *that*.

"Nice name," says Julie, striding along, head high. "You live here forever? Never move? Never have to leave your friends?"

"Yep. Here forever."

"Sheesh! Must be great!"

Lida thinks she'd have no difficulty leaving Tiffany, George, Helena. And their disciples. But already she's dreading the departure of Julie, the big van arriving to remove the bicycle, the birdcage, the piano.

"That's the school," says Lida, as they turn the corner onto Tower Road. "Old. Big and old," she says. "But interesting. Not just a bunch of corridors and doors. I like it." She hasn't known until this moment that she likes the school, but she does. She loves the woodwork and the old banisters and the high windows. In recognizing that love, something stiff and frozen inside her turns soft and spongy.

"Meet me after school?" asks Julie. "We can walk home together. Maybe you can show me things."

"Where? Where'll we meet?" Lida can't believe this is happening to her. She's smiling, because she can't help it. All those beautiful teeth. Dimples.

"Right here, by the parking lot."

"Okay." But of course Julie won't be there. By that time, Tiffany will have her clutches into her. Or Helena. Grabbing Julie as a friend. Telling her about Lider Snider. A shadow passes over Lida's face. Gone are the million-dollar teeth, the dimples, the sparkling eyes.

"You sure?" The perfect Julie looks worried. "You don't have to. I know the way. What's the matter?"

"Nothing." Lida forces a thin smile. "Honest. I'll be here, waiting. No matter what."

"Thanks, Lida," says Julie, as they walk past the parking lot, past the imposing front door of the old school, into the large bare playground. Lida takes her inside and deposits her at the principal's office.

❧

Fifteen minutes later, all eyes are on Julie, as the principal brings her into the classroom to introduce her. "From Victoria, British Columbia," he says. "I hope you'll all make her feel welcome."

What they're all doing is watching her. Making Julie feel welcome will depend on their assessment of her. She and the principal and their teacher, Mrs. Jolliffe, have a little conflab at the front of the room, exchanging papers and records, saying a few quiet words. With eyes narrowed, the kids are sizing Julie up. The boys are thinking: too tall. Most of them are shorter than she is and are waiting impatiently for their first big growth spurt. They're also thinking: too bad. Because Julie has about her a quiet sureness that they find intriguing.

The girls are inspecting Julie even more carefully, trying to decide whether she's going to be a threat, an ally, a pain, a victim, a friend. Most of them opt for friendship, without even conferring with one another, hoping she'll reciprocate. They like her serious, unassuming confidence. They're disappointed when the teacher places her at an empty desk beside Lida.

Mrs. Jolliffe opens the day with a spelling bee. Julie is the first to be chosen for Jeanie's team. They don't know for certain if she can spell, but surely anyone who looks that good can't be a bad speller. They're right. She's good.

Lida is chosen thirteenth by Hugh, but Julie doesn't seem to notice.

Next comes a class on creative writing. Mrs. Jolliffe faces the class and smiles. "This morning," she says, "we're going to learn about similes." She turns around and writes SIMILE on the board. "Pronounced *similee*," she says. "If any of you wants to become a famous author, you'll have to understand about similes. Does anyone know what they are?"

She waits expectantly, but no one replies. Lida can see Julie's hand move ever so slightly above the desk. *She knows,* thinks Lida, but she doesn't want to make a spectacle of herself. She doesn't want to look like a brain, or pushy, on her very first day. Lida thinks she knows what a simile is, too, but there's no way her hand is going to be the only one to shoot up. She runs her thumb and forefinger up and down her pencil and waits.

"You use a simile when you want to say that something is like something else," says Mrs. Jolliffe. She turns again and writes on the board:

The pansy bloom is like a little face.

My kitten is like a gymnast, leaping and tumbling.

"See?" she says.

They all nod, whether they understand or not.

"It's a way of explaining or describing something. Of making it more vivid."

She pauses, to let the idea sink in.

"All right, class," she says. "Now you're all going to do it. Take out your notebooks and write down one thing—

or an animal, maybe—and one person. The person can be real or imaginary. It might be a member of your family, or possibly a friend. Then make up a simile for each one. I'll give you ten minutes. If you finish before then, write some more similes about the thing you have chosen. Or the person. Remember, now: the thing or person is like something else. *Similar* to something else."

There's a lot of pencil-biting, quite a bit of sighing. But most of them are soon bent over their desks, writing. Their scratching pens and the ticking clock are the only sounds in the room.

Lida writes: "The lobster looks like a monster insect, creeping across the rocks on his scary legs." She's seen them crawling around the tank at Sobey's. Then: "My neighbour has a face like a prune—all lines and wrinkles. Her hands are like the crooked branches of a tree. She is very old." Lida's enjoying doing this. It's fun.

Time passes, and the ten minutes are soon up. "Now," says Mrs. Jolliffe, "we're going to read our similes aloud. George, would you start, please?"

George blushes, but he stands up and starts to read: "My canary is like a fat opera singer in a yellow costume."

"Your second one?"

"My mom is like a soft cushion."

Up and down the aisles, Mrs. Jolliffe calls on this one and that one to read. Some of the similes are surprisingly lovely, some boring, some funny, some not really similes at all.

"Now, Julie," says Mrs. Jolliffe. "Let's hear yours."

Julie stands up. She looks at least fourteen, although she's only twelve. She reads slowly, carefully.

"A summer day is like a symphony. The birds are like the instruments—starting, stopping, playing together."

"And your person?"

Julie reads:

"My friend Lida is like a water lily, lying quietly on the surface of the lake, her petals pale and perfect. Her eyes are green, like the still waters of the pond, shining clear and deep in the sunlight."

In the silence that follows, heads snap up from the desks, not sure whether to laugh or to sneer, not sure which is the most acceptable. But it appears that neither option is admissible. The cool and coveted Julie is not laughing, is not sneering. She's looking up from her notebook and smiling quietly at Lida. And yes, she's right. Lida's skin is pale and perfect, her eyes wide open with amazement, and as green as the sea. No one else in the class has green eyes. Even the perfect Tiffany is feeling a sudden dissatisfaction with her own colourless grey ones, forgetting for a moment that they're fringed with a delicious tangle of dark lashes.

In the afternoon, Julie and Lida meet at the corner of the parking lot. As Tiffany and her gang pass by, Tiffany shouts, "Hi, Julie! Hi, Lida!" The day is still foggy and grey. The groaner buoy continues to send out its mournful sound. But to Lida, the day is shot through with the brightest of colours—vermilion, cobalt blue, the sunniest of yellows. The song of the groaner buoy is one she will always love, from this day forward. For better, for worse.

"Want to come into my house for a while?"

"Sure." The veranda with spools on the banisters. The fresh paint. The birdcage.

"What's in the birdcage?"

"In what?"

"In the birdcage. I saw the movers carry it in."

Julie grins. "A bird, of course, dummy." But Julie's *dummy* word is okay. It's not like *Lider Snider* or *stupid face*. It's a comfortable little insult. Lida smiles.

"Don't dummy *me*," she says lightly. "What *kind* of a bird?"

"A canary."

"Like George's opera singer?"

"Yeah." They both laugh.

There are a lot of cartons piled around in Julie's front hall, but already the house looks beautiful. There are ornaments on the mantel and logs piled up in the fireplace. The canary is hopping from one little trapeze to another. The piano stands to the left of the doorway, waiting to be played.

"Can you play it?" Lida looks at Julie.

"Sort of. Just easy stuff. Cliff is the musical one."

"Cliff?"

"My brother. He's in high school. Grade ten. He thinks he's Mr. Wonderful. But I like him. You will, too."

"I wish I had a brother. Or *something*. A sister would be even better."

Julie's mother comes down the long stairway with a stack of towels. She's tall, and she's wearing jeans and a shirt that's much too big for her.

"Hi, sweetie," she says to Julie, kissing her on the cheek. She smiles at Lida. "A new friend," she says, "and here I am in your father's old painting shirt. Hi." And holds out her hand to Lida, clutching the towels with the other. "I'm Julie's mother."

"Hi. I'm Lida." Mrs. Halloway's hand is large and warm, with very long fingers.

"I haven't any nice cookies yet, Julie. Just some of those stale old fig bars from the trip. Help yourselves, kids. Nice to meet you, Lida. Excuse the mess."

Then she's gone, off to the basement on some errand or other.

Julie's never been in a house like this. Shiny floors in the hall, deep carpets in the living room and in the dining room. Silver goblets in the china cabinet. A single ornate candlestick in the centre of the table. The smell of soap and furniture polish. Pictures already on the walls. Real paintings. Lida can tell. She can see the brushstrokes.

"Maybe we can go to your house after school tomorrow," says Julie.

There's a small silence.

"Yes," says Lida, her breathing constricted, her chest hard as concrete.

On the way home, Lida is worried, but she walks tall, and a smile tugs at the sides of her mouth. Even when she enters her tiny house and steps over the boxes of beer in the front porch, even when she sees her father dozing on the sofa, bolt upright, a bottle of beer in his hand, even when she sees her mother's frown as she stirs some concoction on the stove, her smile is struggling to come alive.

"I have a new friend!" she bursts out to her mother, the smile complete and dazzling.

Mrs. Snider is astonished. It must be months, years, since she has seen Lida look like this. Skidding across her mind comes a picture of Lida, eight Christmases ago, opening her first teddy bear—the one thing she'd asked for—her face crazed with joy. Mrs. Snider feels her own spirits lift as she absorbs Lida's smile, her eyes sparked with light. *My daughter.* Forgotten are the stockroom boxes, the smell of dust, the heavy lifting, the long ride home on the buses.

"Her name is Julie. She lives in a big house on Inglis Street. She seems to like me. She says I'm like a water lily. We had fig bars at her house. Her mother was unpacking towels." Lida pauses. Then she continues. "She wants to come over to my house tomorrow."

As she adds the last remark, Lida's perkiness evaporates. She's seeing how drab, how messy her house is. She looks at her father sleeping on the sofa in the next room, his head now lolling on his chest. She counts the bottles on the floor beside him. She looks imploringly at her mother. *Make it okay. Please make it okay.*

Mrs. Snider feels something unfamiliar or long-forgotten stir within her. "I've got some chocolate chips in the cupboard. I haven't forgotten how to make a mean chocolate chip cookie. They'll be better than those fig bars. We've got Coke in the fridge. After supper, you and I will neat up the place a bit. It'll be fine. You'll see." She gives Lida a little pat. Not a hug, but nice all the same.

Lida is feeling almost all right, now. She's remembering about the water lily. She's recalling how the kids were looking at her differently—as though she was *there*. She's sensing again the way her body felt during English class—like she owned it, and that it was good. When she gets old enough to move away from home to a new city or neighbourhood, she's going to call herself Lily. She'll write LIDA on a piece of paper, seal it in an envelope, and mail it to the moon.

Her father is awake, rubbing his eyes. He has a hangover, and he's feeling the weight of regret that usually attacks him upon his re-entry into the conscious world. He has a bad headache, but he sees clearly. What he sees is Lida standing in front of him, looking unlike herself. He can feel waves of energy and urgency emanating from her. She's actually smiling.

"Dad," she is saying, "I have a new friend. She likes me. I went to her beautiful house on Inglis Street today. She has a birdcage and a canary and they have a piano. She said I was like a water lily." She sits down beside him and puts her hand on his knee. "She wants to come over to our house tomorrow afternoon, after school. Dad?"

"Yes?"

"I was wondering. Could you . . . would it be possible . . . ?" She sighs. And adds, "This is important to me, Dad."

He closes his eyes and rubs three fingers back and forth across his forehead. It's quite a while before he stops doing this.

"Yes," he says, finally, his voice uneven. "Yes, I think I can manage it. I'll certainly try. And if I can't, I'll go upstairs and walk into the bedroom and close the door. She won't even know I'm in there." He looks hard at her face. Then he reaches over and hugs her across the shoulders. "My green-eyed beauty," he says. "You're gonna be a knockout by the time you're sixteen."

Stupid face. Dumb. Green-eyed beauty. A knockout by the time you're sixteen. A water lily. Pale and perfect.

Lida floats upstairs to the cracked full-length mirror. She smiles at herself and likes what she sees. How can all this have happened so quickly? Best not to ask. And best, also, to jump very high and fast tomorrow, during dodge ball. If she's picked last again, that's okay. *She'll show them.* That, too, can change.

Apparently anything can.

Two Diaries

Richard

Thursday, April 3

My Mom gave me this diary on my sixteenth birthday. (That was in February and this is April.) But I never opened it up till today. It kind of pissed me off that she gave it to me. She's what's called a *journalist,* which means that she writes stuff for newspapers and magazines and things. Usually she writes about news and maybe just *events,* but sometimes she gets carried away and writes articles about things like Anger Management, or Spousal Abuse, or Drugs in the Teen World. Those are the titles of three of her recent articles. Fortunately, she uses her maiden name when she writes. That way I can pretend I don't even know her. I heard some of the hotshot kids in grade twelve laughing about her article "Drugs in the Teen World." One of the guys said, "This Sheila Carruthers lady sure doesn't have any kids. Otherwise she might know what she's talking about." How do you think I'd have felt if they'd known that Sheila Carruthers was *my mother?* My mother: Sheila Wilcox, married to Trevor Wilcox, the big-wheel, workaholic, obsessive-compulsive lawyer with Henderson, MacArthur, Crosco and Wilcox.

Why was I pissed off by this gift? This huge, 8½ x 11, one-inch-thick hardcover book full of lined paper with my name in gold letters on the front? Well, first of all, listen to what she said. "For you, Richard. To keep track of your life. To record your youth. For blowing off steam. For writing down your hopes and dreams. Enjoy!" Jeez! Enjoy? These are the words of a woman who is crazed with curiosity. Everyone knows that writers—even *fiction* writers—are big-time nosy. But *journalists*—they're sniffing around for news the whole goddamn time. Or views— like, for instance, about a teenager's hopes and dreams. Besides, Mom can't stand it that I keep my life all locked up inside me—wrapped in a tight little bundle, sealed with that tape you use for crating pianos.

I like my mother, I really do. And her spaghetti is just as good as Mrs. Palermo's, Joey Palermo's mom's. But I don't trust her. Anyone who is that chronically worried about her son and only child could never resist the desire to sneak a peek at his diary.

Worried, you ask? Not just nosy? Yes, fuller of anxiety than a nuthatch in a backyard full of cats. She thinks

I'm too quiet. She thinks reading books all the time is
unhealthy, and maybe even suspicious. It makes her
nervous that I'm forever *humming*. And in my bedroom—
alone—picking out my own tunes on my guitar. Why
don't I talk about girls, about football, about where I
want to go to college? The answer to that, Mom (in case
you find this under the pile of gym clothes on the floor of
my closet), is that I'm scared blue of girls, I hate football,
and I'm not even positive I want to go to college. What I
really want to do is be a musician, but my dad can tell you
pretty fast that there's no money in *that*. But college or
not, I sure never want to study to be a lawyer. There you
are, Mom. If you've read this far, you're going to be
uneasy about reading any farther. In any case, I'm going
downtown tomorrow afternoon with my accumulated
allowance money, to buy me a nice big strong metal box
with a lock. Sometimes moms—even journalist moms—go
in your closet and scoop up your sweaty old gym clothes
and toss them into the washer. And there, on the floor,
would be that big black book, staring Mom in the face,
with the words "Richard O'Sullivan Wilcox" written on
the cover in the purest of gold. No, ma'am. I need a
strongbox with a key. RW

Friday, April 4

   I got the box. It cost a lot of money, but it's my insur-
ance policy. I keep it under the bed. That's going to *really*
make Mom into a four-star lunatic. She'll know exactly

what's in that box, and she's going to be tearing her hair out by the roots with frustration and curiosity—and maybe even *fear*. She's going to think that the pages of information I'm hiding in that box are full of lurid secrets of world-class magnitude. Would my dad be worried? No way. I'd fall over dead if he ever even said, "Hi, Richard. How was your day?" He's too busy. Mom's the one who knows I'm alive. But she knows it too *hard*. I keep the key to the box around my neck, day and night, in and out of the shower. RW

Saturday, April 5

I wouldn't want to admit it to Mom, but I'm liking this. This writing stuff down. English is the only subject I got really good marks in this year, so writing isn't a big mountain to climb. I don't have to rev myself up to do it or sweat over the process. In a diary you don't have to be careful of grammar and punctuation and tenses and that other dumb stuff. I can spell *cannibal* C A N I B L E, and no one will ever know—in case I happen to want to talk about one.

I do kind of want to talk about Erika Sandhurst. She's got some Swedish blood in her veins, which I think is really neat. One day when I mentioned her little brother, Olan, my dad, who'd decided he had time to have lunch with us that weekend, said, "Seigrid Sandhurst does the maintenance work on my car at the garage." That's all he said. He sort of *disposed* of Mr. Sandhurst with that sentence. I thought, well, I guess if I decide to marry Erika, there'll be big problems. Dad and Mr. Sandhurst won't be playing golf at the country club. Mrs. Sandhurst and Mom won't be doing the Junior League caper. Christmas dinner will be really tense.

Which is too bad, because as I write this, I'm suddenly 100% certain that that's exactly what I intend to do. I intend to marry Erika Sandhurst. But Dad doesn't have to start worrying yet. The wedding isn't going to happen tomorrow. I haven't even figured out yet how to say hello to her. And sixteen isn't exactly what anyone would call marrying age. RW

Sunday, April 6

I hate Sundays. No school, no Erika to look at in assembly or in the cafeteria. Church in the morning. Lunch with Mom. Sometimes Dad's there too, but usually he's boning up on some case and can't take the time. He's a *criminal lawyer*. He does his best to keep murderers and rapists and burglars on the street and out of jail. I said that to him once, when he was looking sort of receptive to conversation. He froze right up tight and said, "If you were wrongly accused of murder, would you want someone to defend you?" I said, "Yes, but sometimes people *see* these criminals doing their awful things. If you know they're guilty, why do you want to defend them?"

He said, "Everyone, *everyone*, needs to be *proven* guilty before they are convicted. The justice system shelters everyone until that happens. I'm *proud* of the work I do. The law protects you and me, as well as the suspected murderer, from unlawful punishment."

Well, maybe he's proud about that. I'm not. Sometimes I wonder about the victims. Maybe a boy gets his head bashed in by a violent parent. Some smart ass lawyer digs a technicality or two out of his bag of tricks, or else pleads for mercy because of an overdose of alcohol or a bad genetic background. No one's out there pleading for the bashed-in head of the boy, who's too dead to stand up for himself anyway. RW

Monday, April 7

When I came out of the library in school today, I looked down the corridor, and coming towards me, with her eyes looking straight ahead, was Erika. She's just walking along and I'm just standing there, but the old testosterone comes pounding through my whole body like a bunch of charging warhorses. I want to scream and yell and maybe knock down the library wall with my fist. Or pick her up and run around the soccer track with her in my arms. I know she can see me, because she's looking this way, but her expression never changes. I don't want her to see the thunder of lust in my eyes, so I look at the floor and hum a few bars of a little tune I made up last week, and after a while she turns the corner and is gone. It wouldn't have been such a catastrophic thing to say "Hi." I mean it wouldn't be like a proposal of marriage or anything. But she looked so kind of *removed* that my throat closed over before I could get anything past my tonsils.

Erika is about five feet four inches tall, and she's thin. But she's not flat. She's got these perky little breasts that you can see even through her very loose baggy sweaters, which she wears over her very tight jeans. She's not gorgeous like Sharon Stone, or anything, but if the two of them were in a room together, I wouldn't even bother looking at Sharon. Erika has these enormous brown eyes with long curling lashes, and she has straight blond hair that's a weird colour—sort of like bleached sand. That's about it: big eyes and blond hair. Plus that faraway, unconnected look that makes me want to fall down in a heap at her feet. RW

Erika

Thursday, April 3
Dear Diary:

I'm glad I got rid of that dinky little pink diary with the brass key. It drove me crazy because of its pinkness, and also because of its smallness. I went over to the convenience store and bought a bunch of Hilroy notebooks. They're skinny, although they have 32 pages. Skinny is good, because it means my diary will be easy to hide. That little pink thing I've been using didn't have enough space in it, but it was *fat*. Fat is hard to hide. I kept it under my mattress, but any mother who was really vigilant could easily have seen that the top of the bed had a little bump on it. Then she'd just *know* there was something important under there. Either my Mom isn't vigilant or else she's really respecting my privacy. But I don't want to take the chance. So mostly I didn't tell really important stuff in that little pink diary. I just said things like, "Got up, was late for gym class, got a B-minus in geometry, listened to Steven Wilson tell me his boring life story in lunch hour, babysat the Keneally kid, did my homework, crashed." I never would have dared to say that I spend my days hoping that I'll see Richard Wilcox. I don't have any big plans about him. I just want to be able to look at him and think about touching his big bony hands. I'd never have dared say that in my little old pink diary.

    Confidentially,

        Erika

Friday, April 4

Dear Diary:

    I feel sort of expansive now that I have room to spread my thoughts all over these big pages. Only 32 pages per notebook, but I bought a whole lot of them. When I finish the next one, I can start putting #2 under the mattress, beside #1. I've measured the mattress. I figure I can keep at least 24 of them under there (one layer) to start out with. Then I can start a new layer. Or maybe I can put them in a big binder, which even a vigilant mother would think was school work. I could maybe write GEOGRAPHY or SOCIAL STUDIES on the cover. I don't think my mom would be interested in poking around a book like that. Mostly she just seems interested in cooking and sewing and making sure that Olan and I are safe and healthy. If she read my diary it would be to make sure that I wasn't getting tangled up with drugs or sleeping around. Why doesn't she just ask me? I could tell her that I'm too shy to even say *hello* to a boy when I like him. I certainly wouldn't be jumping into his bed or doing drugs with him. Richard spends so much time in the school library that I don't know if he even *has* a bed. Maybe he sleeps in the library in the Music and Memories section. Or on the Fiction and Fantasy shelf. I like books, too. And not just reading them.

    Goodnight,

        Erika

Saturday, April 5
Dear Diary:

    On Saturdays, Mom works at Sears, in the catalogue department. So I have to babysit Olan (who is eight, Mom and Dad's little afterthought) and get supper ready. If I go to the mall or anything, I have to take Olan with me. Fun city. I'd like to just sort of hang out and watch the people, or maybe go check out the diamond rings, but Olan wants to be *going* somewhere all the time. He never stays in one place long enough for me to put down roots. When we stop for a hot chocolate, I can do my heavy looking. I love watching people. They make me think of stories. I want to be a writer. Maybe when he's old, Richard will read my books. I love to think of him tenderly turning the pages.

    Happy Saturday,

        Erika

Sunday, April 6
Dear Diary:

It's snowing today. What a stupid climate. In Ontario, where we used to live, you could sometimes have a sunbath in April. In Nova Scotia, it's different. Not that anyone can enjoy the sun anymore. A parent is always rushing out to cover you with sunscreen. In the old days, my hair used to get so bleached by the sun that it would be almost white, and my skin would get really brown. Even at ten years old, I could see that I looked pretty cool. Now I look like I have leukemia, or some rare blood disease that has sucked all the red blood cells out of me.

I spent the afternoon with Pamela Dorino. She's my best friend. We don't have any secrets from each other. Except I don't tell her about Richard, and I don't know why. She tells me about Chuck O'Donnell, and even about what they do in the high grasses behind Bayswater beach. How could I explain that Richard and I haven't even *spoken* to each other?

When I came home, Mom and Dad were sitting on the sofa, holding hands and watching a movie on TV. Olan was spending the night at Georgie's house. My mom and dad really like one another. I think my father is almost perfect. He's a garage mechanic at that huge building downtown where all the big cheeses have their offices—engineers and lawyers and some high-power doctors. He looks after their car repairs and maintenance. He's in love with his work. To him a car engine is like a human body that needs to be kept healthy and beautiful, and has to be cured if it gets sick or broken. He says he feels like a doctor. He even says he's *diagnosing* a car when he's trying to discover the cause of a rattle or a thump or a hiccup in the engine. I envy him, because he loves what he's doing with his life. I hope I can be like that someday. Right now I want to be an author, but usually writers don't make much money. If I don't get married, I'll have to have some way to pay the rent. I don't want to marry any of the boys who phone me up all the time. They're either boring or stoned or have itchy fingers. Reg Stuart and Jimmy Doyle and Hampton McCulloch all called me tonight. I said No to all of them. Reg is boring, Jimmy is usually stoned, and Hampton has itchy fingers. The one I want is Richard. I went upstairs and read *Fall on Your Knees*.

Frustrated,

Erika

Monday, April 7

Dear Diary:

Today I saw Richard. I was walking down the corridor from my home room when all of a sudden I saw him coming out of the library. He looked down the hall, and he must have seen me, because I was all alone. It was four o'clock, and everyone else was at play practice. He just sort of *stopped*. He didn't go forward or back, and when I got really close, he started looking at the floor, or his feet, and also humming a really bouncy tune that made me feel like dancing or something. Is there something *wrong* with me, or what? He could have said hi or smiled, don't you think? I couldn't speak to someone who was having a conversation with the floor, could I?

Sometimes I think I can feel him staring at me—like in assembly or in the cafeteria—but when I look over at him, his eyes slide off me and focus on empty space. Why do I have to be having all these wild ungovernable feelings for someone who's so weird? When I was walking by him, at the library door, I wanted to leap up and throw my arms around him and hug him until his head almost fell off. Maybe *that* would have made him take his eyes off the floor. But (sigh!) maybe not.

And what about that tune he was humming? It wasn't familiar, but even in just a quiet little hum it was so catchy that I wanted to skip down the hall to it. If we could ever get to the "hello" stage, I could ask him what it was. But I'm beginning to think that's never going to happen.

Gloomily,

Erika

Richard

Tuesday, April 8

Listen to what happened today. I had some stuff to do downtown after school this afternoon (guitar strings, a book to return to the library) and it was really late when I finished. So I decided I'd go over to Dad's office and check out if maybe he was coming home to dinner. The snow had stopped and the rain was coming down in buckets. I figured I wouldn't turn down a drive. "Okay," says he when I poke my head in his door. "I just finished a brief. Go get my car and pick me up at the front door. It's in the garage, having the snow tires removed."

All the way to the garage, I'm thinking, "Don't let this happen to me. Let someone else be working on that car. Don't let it be Mr. Sandhurst." And of course it is. I've never met him before, but the minute I see him I know he's Erika's father. He's on the phone and he's writing on a big schedule that's tacked to the wall, but he's facing in my direction. Good cheekbones. A lot of faded blond hair. Blue eyes, but they're shaped just like hers. Long fingers. I just stand there like a piece of meat, staring at him talking, until he hangs up. Then he looks me in the eye, and says, "Well?" He has a nice deep voice. I say, "I came to pick up my dad's car. It's black. Mr. Wilcox's car. I'm his son. It's a Cadillac." It's like I'm a babbling brook. I can't stop talking. Do I think he doesn't know which one is Mr. Wilcox's car?

He's watching me really carefully. Then he says, "You look so much like him that I guess you have to be his son. Can't be handing over a Cadillac to every kid that says his father owns one."

I laugh. "I guess not," I say. "Could be a nice easy way to get a new car." Then I dig out my driver's licence and show it to him.

He laughs, too. I sign a paper, saying I've picked the car up. Then he tosses me the keys and says, "Tell your dad there's a murmur in the engine that I think I should look into. Not serious. But not my idea of good, either. Bye, Richard." And off I go. "Bye, Mr. Sandhurst," I say, over my shoulder. I liked him. For a father-in-law, he'll do fine. RW

Erika

Tuesday, April 8
Dear Diary:

I'm weak in the knees tonight. I went to the garage so I could bum a ride home with Dad after my gymnastics lesson at the Y, and who was in there with him? I nearly fainted. Richard! Talking to Dad. They were laughing! Then Dad threw him a bunch of keys, and Richard drove off in the biggest, blackest Cadillac you ever saw. I can't stand it. He laughs and talks with my *father*. He won't even say hi to *me*. He's *rich*. I'm *not*. I want to go shut myself in my room and never come out.

That Hampton McCulloch of the itchy fingers keeps pestering me. He sometimes nudges up to me when I'm getting stuff out of my locker, and sort of brushes his hand across my breasts. He also says lewd things to me. I don't even want to tell my *diary* exactly what he says. In between the obscenities, he says stuff like, "So, how's Miss Prissy today? Are you gonna be a little Goody Two-Shoes all your life? Don't you ever want to have some *fun?*" Then he says more gross things. I can feel myself getting redder and hotter in the face, and when I try to close my locker, he puts his foot in the door. I know why there are battered women, but no battered men. The only reason is that women aren't big enough or strong enough. If I'd been able to do it, I would

have taken Hampton McCulloch's big fat face and slammed it
right into the wall. That's how crazy mad I was.

In fury,

Erika

Richard

Wednesday, April 9

Today I had to go back to the school to get my geometry notebook, which I left behind in the classroom. I
forgot we had homework. It was quiet in the school until
I got near the corner of the corridor where our lockers are.
Then I heard a scuffling noise and some grunts and sounds
that were sort of like squeals. When I came around the
corner, there they were—Hampton McCulloch and Erika
Sandhurst. He's got a big knee between her legs and a
hand over her mouth. With the other hand he's pinching
her breast. Ever hear the expression "I saw red"? Well—*I
saw it*. I ploughed into old Hampton like he was a
Volkswagen beetle and I'm a Mack truck. I don't even
know what I did to him. All I know is that suddenly he's
running down the corridor so fast that you couldn't catch
him with a motorcycle. Erika's crouched down on the
floor with her gorgeous pale hair all tangled up, and she's
making strangled little animal noises. When she finally
stands up, her nose is running and her mouth is screwed
up and she's sobbing, really loud. I go over and put my
arms around her and tell her it's okay. On Monday I

couldn't even say "Hi" to her. Today I'm hugging her like it's the most natural thing I ever did. While this is going on, I'm feeling sad for her, but I'm feeling so happy for me that I guess I must have a split personality. Then I take her home. Hand in hand, like in all the best stories. Tomorrow we're going to the school play together. On the weekend I'm going to teach her how to play the guitar. I almost feel grateful to Hampton McCulloch. But he doesn't know how lucky he is that he can run really fast. RW

Erika

Wednesday, April 9
Dear Diary:

I feel kind of peculiar tonight, so I won't write very long. Mom says it's shock. Shock? You better believe it.

I was in the library doing research for my project on the Aztecs. I was all alone in there except for the volunteer librarian. The only kids in the school were in the auditorium for a dress rehearsal of tomorrow's play. Once I looked up and saw Hampton McCulloch slink by the door, but as soon as I saw him I put my head right down. No way was I going to have eye contact with that miserable jerk. He's doing backstage work on the play, so I guess he was running an errand or something for the stage manager. He was carrying a big box.

Well, finally I got all the information I needed for my project—lots of facts, plus photocopies of some great pyramids and ruins and beautiful chunky sculptures. I stuck it all in my backpack and started off for my locker to get my jacket. Standing right beside it, with a big ugly smirk on his face, was Hampton. I pretended he wasn't there, and marched right up to open my locker. He pushed me aside and got between me and my coat. I was a little bit spooked, but mostly I was just grossed out. He said, "I think you're ready to have a little fun." Then he took my arm, and squeezed it so hard that tonight I can still see his nail marks on my skin. After that, he yanked me really close and put his left arm around my neck and his hand over my mouth. Now I was so scared that I felt paralyzed. Then he stuck his stupid knee between my legs and pressed really hard. As soon as he got me in that position where I couldn't move a muscle and couldn't scream, he started playing with my right breast—squeezing it, pinching it, poking it. And telling me what he planned to do next.

Then, all of a sudden, when I was right in the middle of thinking I wanted to die, this person stormed over and yanked him away. Then he took Hampton by the arm and swung him so fast that he slammed across the corridor into a bunch of metal lockers, whamming his forehead so hard that it bled. Hampton didn't stick around to discuss the weather. He took off down the hall like he was pursued by a locomotive. I was on the floor, shaking like a Slinky toy, but I could see everything through my fingers. I also discovered that it was *Richard* who was standing there. He bent over to help me stand up, and as soon as I was more or less vertical, he put his arms around me and said, in this wonderful quiet voice, "It's okay." I was crying out loud with my mouth open and my nose running, but I didn't care. I was feeling like I was going to burst wide open with terror and relief and amazement and joy. Then he took my hand and walked me home and deposited me into the arms of my mother. He also told her what happened, because I still couldn't speak.

Later on, I phoned him up and said thank you for rescuing me from a fate worse than death. I was feeling better by then, so we talked a long time. It was like our taps were turned on and we couldn't stop. He's taking me to the school play tomorrow night. He wants to be a musician. If he gets to be a musician and I become a writer and we get married, we'll starve to death. But starvation never looked so good.

Goodnight, Diary. I'm getting very sleepy.

Your friend,

Erika

P.S. He's going to teach me to play the guitar.

P.P.S. He writes songs that are really just tunes, because he can't write the lyrics for them. Guess who's going to start putting words to those songs.

Fathers

It was the last day of school. Not just the last day of school before the holidays. This was the *very* last day of school. In fact, school was really already over. They were just there to pick up their marks and check that their lockers were empty. This afternoon, at three P.M. sharp, would be their graduation ceremony. They'd come marching into the auditorium in those stupid sea-blue gowns. Jeff Sangster was eighteen. He'd just discovered that he'd placed second in his class. The person who came first—a *girl,* for crying out loud—would get the gold medal. No medal for the person who came second. Just a goddamn book or something. But that was okay. He didn't care. Stupid medal. You couldn't even wear it. Who'd want it?

Mrs. Galaxy, their homeroom teacher, was standing behind her desk, ready with her parting words. "It will be exciting, sometimes frustrating, but always interesting. You'll be setting out on a quest, which won't come to an end until you are lowered into the ground in your own coffin." Thus spake Mrs. Galaxy, a woman who must have been ninety-nine if she was a day.

Well! A coffin.

Fingers Delaney spoke up. He was called Fingers because he had six fingers on his left hand—five fingers, to be exact, and one thumb. But nobody held that against him, not even his steady girlfriend, who seemed to think he was the next thing to being perfect. Fingers was the class comedian and the class spanner. Spanner? It's what gets thrown into the works in order to confuse the machinery. But Fingers had been holding himself in for six weeks. He was smart—not smart enough to get that gold medal, but clever enough to see through anything that was phony or hypocritical or pompous or dumb. He questioned everything, even simple things. If someone said, "It's going to be sunny all day. The Bedford weatherman says so," you could expect Fingers to say, "To begin with, it was a weather*woman* this morning, and, to continue, I'd ask you to check the sky." Sure enough, there'd be a large black cloud moving slowly toward them from the east and a big fog bank inching up from the harbour. And if a teacher was making a false or obscure state-ment, Fingers Delaney would be the first one to question it. But if you're that smart, you know that you start to soften your blows or even pull your punches before and during exam season. Yes sir. No sir. Yes ma'am. No ma'am. That was the route to go until the territory was safe again. It would never be safer than on this last day of school.

The exams were over; the die was cast. No marks could be added or taken away. Fingers had come sixth out of twenty-eight, which suited him just fine. He was off to journalism school in the fall, and if there was anything he planned to do with his future, it was to tell it like it is. No phony stuff to shock or titillate or manipulate his readers or listeners or watchers. Just plain unadorned truth.

He wanted that now. "A quest, eh?" His smile spread over his handsome face. "And what kind of quest might that be, Mrs. Galaxy?" Smart alecky, but not mean. The kids loved him. He was the most popular guy in the class.

"I was about to tell you, Charles." (Mrs. Galaxy referred to him as Fingers in the staff room, but not in the classroom.) "The quest for self-knowledge. The lifelong journey to discover who you really are."

There was a silence. Even with the exams over and Mrs. Galaxy due to retire next year, no one was sure how to handle this one. Even if Mrs. G. wasn't a nut case, that was a pretty crazy statement.

She smiled. "Or perhaps you don't agree. Possibly you think you've already got that all worked out. I'd be interested in your opinions."

Jeff Sangster squirmed in his seat. What she was saying was a big load of malarkey, but if he came right out and said so, she might think he was mad because he hadn't placed first. Which wasn't the case. Dammit, he didn't care.

He coughed. "I think I know who I am right now," he said.

"Ah!" said Mrs. Galaxy. "Good for you, Jeff. That's going to save you a lot of hard thinking and some fruitless agonizing. I'm sixty-four years old and I discover some new and surprising thing about myself at least once a week. And I don't always like what I discover."

Fingers frowned. This wasn't the first time he'd heard one or another version of the expression "Know thyself." Like Jeff, he figured he knew exactly who he was. He not only knew who he was now, he thought he had a pretty clear idea of who he was going to be in ten years' time. He put up his hand, the one with the correct number of fingers on it.

"Yes, Charles."

"I don't think I understand any of that stuff, Mrs. Galaxy. What's so hard about knowing yourself? Sounds easy to me."

"It's not." Mrs. Galaxy sounded 100 percent sure of what she was talking about. "It's the hardest thing in the world."

Jeff looked at the floor. He wished this crazy discussion would stop so he could get home in time to take a shower before lunch. When he got this hard knot in his stomach, a long hot shower had a way of easing it out. What knot? Well, he didn't know. But it was there, gnawing away at him. And Fingers was prolonging this senseless conversation. "Why?" he was saying.

"Because all of us are complicated, evasive, rationalizing, procrastinating, and altogether imperfect people.

Who we are isn't just our names and where we live and whether or not we're tall or short, or smart or not-so-smart, or beautiful or ordinary, or happy or sad. It's knowing exactly how we feel about all those things, and whether or not our perception of ourselves is accurate."

Fingers was genuinely puzzled. And also genuinely interested. But before he could ask his next question, Rosalee Morana spoke up.

"Mrs. Galaxy," she started, clearing her throat, "would it be okay to ask you about one of those things that you learned about yourself during the past month?"

Mrs. Galaxy paused, but only for a moment. "Sometimes," she said, "it's hard to come face to face with those truths, even in the privacy of your own mind. To share them with other people is a hurdle of a different kind." She paused again, rubbing a spot behind her ear. "But I think maybe I'm going to try to do it."

Now she had the attention of the whole class. If this was confession time, they wanted to hear every word. Even Jeff forgot about his shower while she continued.

"The fact that I find this hard to do is one of the things I'm discovering about myself today. I had thought I was open and direct, ready to share my thoughts with anyone who was willing to listen. Well, it appears that this is not the case. I can see that I'd really like to keep some of my shortcomings locked away inside, so that you could walk into graduation this afternoon with the same attitude toward me that you had yesterday. I'd like to keep my mask on. Well—let's take it off."

Fingers looked troubled. "You don't have to do this, you know, Mrs. Galaxy."

"C'mon, Mrs. Galaxy," urged Rosalee. "Then maybe we'd know what you're talking about."

"Thanks, Charles," said Mrs. Galaxy, "but Rosalee's right. Besides, I'm not about to confess to murder or robbery or cheating on my income tax. But here—here are three brand new things I've learned about myself during the past month."

She sat down and faced them from across the desk. "Two weeks ago, I was soaking in the tub when all of a sudden a memory popped right into my head."

Jeff didn't like thinking about Mrs. Galaxy soaking in that tub. He tried to concentrate on what she was saying. He hoped it was a bubble bath, so that she'd be covered up.

"It was a memory about something that happened fifteen years ago. It was when I was teaching a grade eight class. I let one of the boys go into grade nine who didn't deserve to pass. I told myself that it would be too hard for him—socially and psychologically—to stay back with students who were so much younger than he was. He was tall and he was sophisticated in a street-smart way. So I let him pass. I felt it was the merciful thing to do. I felt *virtuous* about it. When the memory appeared to me in the bathtub that night, I knew that I'd been hiding something for fifteen years. Not just deceiving my principal. Fooling myself, too. I remembered what a troublemaker that boy had been, how cruel and mean-minded he was. And even in grade eight, he couldn't keep his hands off the girls in the class. Forever pinching their behinds. *I didn't want to have him in my class for another year.* So I passed him. I know that he dropped out of school in the middle of grade nine, and disappeared from the town. The grade was probably far too hard for him. I may have wrecked his life." She paused. "This wasn't a good piece of myself to look at. This wasn't an aspect of self-knowledge that I welcomed."

No one said anything. Jeff was hoping that Mrs. Galaxy's next memory wouldn't reveal itself in the bathtub. It didn't.

"A week or so later, I was looking at myself in my full-length mirror. Fixing my hair or something. And I looked at my ankles. All my life—ever since I was a scared and awkward child of eleven—I've known that I had thick ankles. *Very* thick ankles. But I told myself I didn't care, that I'd get by on my black eyes and curly hair and energetic personality. And maybe I did. I certainly had lots of boyfriends and girlfriends. But when I looked at them in the mirror that day, I could see how terrible those ankles were, how they made my legs look like fat posts of wood, how no one could ever, ever be a showstopper with those legs. And I knew then that I'd been lying to myself when I'd said so often that I didn't care about my ankles. In a small part of my mind, I was always conscious of them. They kept me from a genuine self-confidence, long after I should have stopped worrying about such nonsense. What's more, I knew I hate, hate, *hated* those legs. Then, sixty-four years old though I am, I sat down on a chair and cried. Cried and cried for all the times I'd wanted to be beautiful and perfect but wasn't. And do you know something strange? That big cry was very healing. I realized that I should have dug out that hidden part of me a long time ago, looked at it, dealt with it, and then put it aside."

Three. Mrs. Galaxy had said that she'd tell them three things. Jeff had stopped worrying about his shower. Fingers was looking more serious than anyone had ever seen him look. Rosalee was trying not to appear as eager as she felt.

"This last one is very hard to tell," said Mrs. Galaxy. "It's about my husband, Eric."

All the students knew that Mrs. Galaxy's husband had been dead for about twenty-five years, that she'd brought up her two children all by herself, that everyone said she was a courageous woman who'd triumphed over most of life's difficult obstacles.

She continued. "Everyone thought I was so brave, with him dying so young, and me having to raise my daughters all by myself. And I did a good job. They are wonderful young women—kind, responsible and independent—each one headed toward the kind of life she wants. All those years, I felt so proud of myself and so heroic, and the whole community thought I was a marvel. Then one day last week I looked through an old photo album. I paused at one picture. There were the girls, smiling and looking especially pretty. In the background, standing in front of the lilac bushes, were Eric and me—both of us looking noticeably unhappy. And then I remembered how much I had grown to dislike him. I recalled his frequent bouts of anger, and how often he unjustly criticized the three of us and made us feel so worthless. And how very charming he was to everyone except the people who lived in his own house; how he ridiculed the way I brought up the girls and undermined my authority. Was I grief-stricken and noble after he died? No, I was *relieved*. I was free to live my life and bring up my kids without that kind of abuse. But I lived that lie for twenty-five years. I *believed* that lie. I agreed with the people who felt sorry for me when my husband was killed in a car accident (full of liquor, I might add), and I agreed with everyone who said I was brave. When I looked at the memory of all that, I knew myself a little better than I had the day before. And it was a grim relief to have that mask stripped from my face."

No one said anything. "It's hard for me to believe," she said with a grin, "that I've actually told you all those ugly things. I've given that little pep talk about knowing yourself to every graduating class on the last day of school. Today, I suddenly couldn't stand it that no one ever seems to know what I'm talking about. Believe me, some of the things I've learned about myself have been good. If I'd told you those things—that I've discovered I'm strong, generous, and a survivor—you still wouldn't have understood what I was trying to tell you. But I think you do now."

She picked up her books and her purse, and looked at the class. "I've liked having you as my homeroom students. I'll probably cry a little tonight when I realize that you've gone out of my care forever. But you've left me with a lot of good memories—serious ones and crazy ones. Now, go home and make yourselves handsome and beautiful for this afternoon."

Jeff walked home alone—slowly. He was thinking about how he wasn't going to get that first-place medal. Well, he didn't care. Stupid old medal. The knot was forming in his midsection again. He took a shortcut through the Public Gardens—nearly empty at this hour— and sat down on a bench. He watched but didn't really see the ducks and the pigeons. He discovered that his throat was tight and that in a subdued kind of way he was crying. *He'd wanted it so much. He'd needed so badly to prove to his father that he was a winner.* He was so sick of being put down, of being told he was a sissy, of being mocked for being a klutz at baseball, of being made to feel like such a big nothing. A medal would have done it—or he'd hoped it would. Now he was just a lousy second, and his father's first remark—he *knew* it—wouldn't be "Congratulations!" It would be "Who got the medal?" Jeff cared about that medal. He cared a whole lot. And if this was knowing yourself, what was so great about it? He frowned and thought hard. Well, for one thing, he was feeling angry at his father instead of hurt. And what's more, if his dad said, "Just *second?*" Jeff knew he was ready to tell him that you had to be really good to come second, and that even if he wasn't exactly what his father wanted him to be, he *was* smart. And that he was worth

a whole lot. If his father laughed at him or insulted him—
if he *humiliated* him—he'd just walk out of the room. And
maybe slam the door.

He got up from the bench and started for home. He still
had time for his shower, but the knot was gone. He could
take a short one, and have more time to get ready for
graduation. Maybe clean his shoes or something. He was
really looking forward to the ceremony. The principal
would announce that he'd placed second, and he'd go up
on the stage to get his prize. There'd be a reception afterwards, and his mom would be wearing that soft blue dress
she kept for special occasions. She'd be so proud of him.
And the dance tonight would be great. Rosalee was the
girl he had his eye on, and he knew she liked him. She kept
looking at him over the top of her looseleaf binder. That
had to mean something.

∽

Fingers Delaney walked along Quinpool Road with his
usual collection of friends scattered around and behind
him. They joked about this and that, threw rocks at trees,
talked a bit about Mrs. Galaxy's revelations.

"I still don't know what she meant," said one of the
girls. "It seems like getting to know yourself means
digging up a whole lot of bad memories, or else looking at
yourself and not liking what you see."

Fingers kicked a pop can along as he walked up
Windsor Street. "Maybe," he said, "but it's more complicated than that. When she was digging around, she found

good stuff too." But he was looking worried. He wasn't fooling around as much as he usually did.

When he reached his house, he didn't invite anyone in for a Coke or a Pepsi or for anything at all. He just walked in, yelled "See you this aft," and disappeared inside. Then he went up to his room, closed the door, and sat down on the edge of his bed. He knew what he had to do. He had to raise his hand and take a long, hard look at those fingers. Thick ankles and fat legs weren't great. But anyone could tell you that having six fingers was worse.

Mostly, he carried on as though that left hand didn't exist. He didn't think about it. When his fingernails were long he cut them, and sometimes he even cleaned them when they were dirty. Not often enough, according to his mother. He grinned at that thought. She wasn't a nagger, but she knew how to tease him—in a nice way. Like: "Your nails look like you've been mining coal all day. Do something about that before supper, eh?" And his dad would just laugh. But no one at home ever spoke about those six fingers. Not even his kid sister, who knew how to be such a pest in other ways—staying forever in the bathroom when he wanted a shower, or using up all the hot water when *she* was having a shower.

So, sure, he knew about those six fingers. It's just that they seemed to exist somewhere else, outside of himself. He never really *looked* at them. He didn't think he tried *not* to look at them. But maybe he did. Otherwise, why was he trying so hard to avoid doing it right now?

Fingers got up and shut his bureau drawer—always open and spilling forth socks and stray pairs of underwear. He picked a book up off the floor and shoved it into the bookcase. He reread the letter from Stanley Helms, who'd moved to Montreal with his family last spring. Fingers checked. Half of it was in French. *Trying to impress me*. Stanley said that Quebecers knew how to have fun. They didn't have to be loaded down with pot or beer in order to have a good time. Then Fingers changed the date on his calendar. After all, this was an important day. He sharpened a couple of pencils. Then he sat down on the bed again and looked at his left hand.

He held it up so that the palm faced him. Then he held up his right hand in the same way and compared them. Well, different, all right, but not outrageously so. The fingers on his left hand were all neatly placed, all beside one another, more or less straight. A person might not notice, unless he was actually counting. Then he turned his left hand over, so that the back was facing him. *Don't kid yourself, Fingers Delaney, that no one's going to notice that!* He was "Fingers" Delaney, wasn't he? He could remember kids teasing him about his fingers one day, in kindergarten or maybe grade one—a long time ago. He'd come home and told his dad. His father had thumped him on the back. "Sure your hand's different from theirs," he'd said. "That makes you special. *Very special*. Don't you ever forget that!" He could recall telling the kids exactly that when he'd gone back to school

after lunch that day. He'd held up his hand and said,
"I'm *special*." Apparently they'd believed it. Apparently
he had.

But he wasn't in grade one anymore. He was in grade
twelve. Finished with grade twelve. How did those
fingers look to him now? He made a fist, and looked at
his hand with the fingers facing him. Suddenly he
laughed out loud. *A lot of fingers.* Then he held his
hand up again with the back facing him. Pretty weird,
certainly. But he'd had that hand for eighteen years. He
hummed a tune from *My Fair Lady:* "I've Grown
Accustomed to Your Face." He was accustomed to that
hand. It was his. "*My hand,*" he said out loud. Fingers
did some more thinking. It seemed, as his father had
said, that the hand made him a little bit special. The kids
at school sometimes made fun of him, but in a friendly
way. If he sank a bunch of baskets in a basketball game,
someone was bound to say, "No wonder he's so good.
He's got more fingers to work with!" And he knew that
his nickname was a real—if odd—mark of esteem. He
knew people liked him.

If given his choice, Fingers would probably have opted
for a normal hand. But he'd looked at it hard today—
remembered some things, thought about others. He
believed that his vision was clear. Insofar as his six fingers
were concerned, he figured that he knew himself—that
aspect of himself, anyway. He grinned his exceedingly
attractive grin and sighed with relief. Something inside
him knew that he'd been avoiding this past half hour of

scrutiny for many years. Now it was over, and it was also okay.

"Thank you, Mrs. Galaxy," said Fingers, as he went off to the bathroom for his pre-graduation shower.

Dreams

I was sixteen years old when he took my dream away from me. It is not a small offence to be a stealer of dreams.

Our family lived in Mackerel Cove, a small fishing village on the South Shore of Nova Scotia. When I tell people that, when I point out the exact location, they look at me with a puzzled, almost incredulous expression. Sometimes that look is all I get. Other times, they give voice to their astonishment. "But how did you become what you are? How did you get from there to here?"

What do they think goes on in small fishing communities? Nothing? Do they assume that such places contain people with no brains, no ambition, no dreams? They look at me as though my skin had just turned green. As though I'd been cast in some inferior mould and had, by some miracle of agility or cussedness, found a way to jump out of it. By the time those questions started, I was a junior executive in an oil company, in the days before oil became a controversial commodity—in Toronto, where the mould is often even more fixed than elsewhere.

When I was a boy of eleven, the horizon was endless, physically and metaphorically. From our yellow frame house—which was perched on a hill, without the protection or impediment of trees—you could view the wide sea, stretching from the rocky point and behind Granite Island, disappearing beyond the edge of the sky, inviting dreams of any dimension. And in the foreground, four reefs threw their huge waves up into the air—wild, free.

I spent a lot of time sitting on the woodpile—when I was supposed to be cutting wood, piling wood, or carting wood—looking at that view. And thinking. Planning. Rumour had it that if you drew a straight line from our front door, right through the centre of that horizon, the line would eventually end up on the west coast of North Africa. How can Torontonians conclude that such an environment is limiting? They're lucky if they can see through the smog to the end of the block. I could go straight from the woodpile to Africa. Or I could turn left and wind up in Portugal.

And the wind. On that hill, where my great-grandfather had had the vision to build his house, the wind was always a factor. Even when it was not blowing. Then my mother would emerge into the sunshine or the fog, and take a deep breath. "Gone," she would announce. She hated the wind. She was from near Truro, where the slow, muddy Salmon River just limps along its banks, shining brown and slithery in the dead air. Dead air—that's what inlanders seem to want. Then they feel safe. Or peaceful. But those were two words that meant nothing to me at that time.

What is it about kids that makes them so blind and deaf for so long? Some of them, anyway. How can they go charging into life with such a certainty that all is well? Without, in fact, a passing thought as to whether it is or is not? It's just there. Mackerel are for jigging, the sea is for swimming, a boat is for rowing around in. The gulls are for watching, particularly on those days when the wind is up, when they just hang high in the air, motionless, wings wide, riding the storm. I was like that when I was eleven, sailing along with no effort, unconscious of the currents and turbulence that surrounded me.

Twelve seems to be a favourite time for waking up. What is so special about twelve that makes it such a hazardous, such a brittle age? No doubt it's partly because of all those puberty things—those unseen forces that begin to churn up your body, making it vulnerable to dangers that didn't even seem to exist before that time. And as with the body, so go the head and the heart.

All of a sudden (it really did seem to start happening all within the space of a day), I began to hear things. Things like the edge in my mother's voice, the ragged sound of my father's anger. Where had I been before? Too busy on the woodpile, in the boats, at the beach—*outside*. Or when inside, shut off by comic books, TV, the all-absorbing enjoyment of food. And lots of arguing and horsing around with my brothers and sisters, of whom there were five. But now, suddenly the wind blew, and I heard it.

Once you have heard those sounds, your ears are permanently unplugged, and you cannot stop them up again. Same thing with the eyes. I began to see my mother's face as an objective thing. Not just *my mother,* a warm and blurry concept, but a face to watch and think about and read. It was pinched, dry-looking, with two vertical lines between the brows. Much of the time, I saw, she looked anxious or disenchanted. I didn't know the meaning of that word, back then, but I recognized the condition. She was thin and pale of skin—probably because she didn't like to be out in the wind—with a head of defeated-looking thin brown hair. I saw that for the first time, too.

Within twenty-four hours of my awakening, I felt that I had discovered and recognized everything. My mother, I knew, was worried about money—or about the extreme scarcity of it. That seemed a waste of time to me. There were fish in the sea, vegetables in the garden, loaves of bread in the oven, and second-hand clothes to be had at Frenchy's. But look again. Not just worry. Something else. And that, I knew, had to do with my father. I watched very carefully. He didn't ask for things. He demanded: "Gimme the sugar." "Let the dog out." "Eat your damn vegetables." He didn't praise. He criticized: "This soup is too cold." "There's a rip in them pants." And on pickling day: "Too blasted hot in this kitchen." As he made each one of these remarks, I would see a small contraction in those vertical lines on my mother's forehead. Not much, but to me it was an electric switch. I was aware of a connection.

With this new and unwelcome knowledge, I watched the other kids to assess their reactions. But they were younger than I was. So there was nothing much to watch. They continued to gabble on among themselves, giggling, pushing, yelling at one another. Even when my father would shout, "Shut up, damn you!" they'd all just disperse, regroup, and continue on as before. Well, not quite all. I focused on Amery, aged seven, eyes wide and bright, chewing on his nails. Awake, too, I thought, and felt a kinship with him.

My father didn't work as a fisherman in our little village. He was employed in the fish plant, gutting fish. Slash and gut, slash and gut, eight hours a day, five days a week, fifty weeks a year. Enough to limit the vision of any Bay Street Torontonian. I heard people in our village talk about what it was like to work with him. "A real jewel of a man," said one woman to my mother. "Patient, and right considerate. Always ready to help out." I looked at Ma while the woman was talking. I was thirteen by then, and very skillful at reading faces. She's struggling, I concluded, to keep the scorn out of her face. It was a fixed mask, telling nothing—except to me. A man friend of Pa's once said to me, "I sure hope you realize how lucky you are to have a father like him. He's some kind. A real soft-spoken man." I said nothing, and adjusted my own mask. When my father had left the house that morning, he'd yelled back at my mother, "Get your confounded books off the bed before I get home tonight! I'm sick of you with your smart ass ways!" Then he'd slammed the door so hard that a cup fell off the shelf.

My dream was a simple one. Or so it may seem to you. I wanted to be the most talented fisherman in Mackerel Cove. Talented! I can see the incredulous looks on the faces of my Toronto colleagues. Do they really think that the profession of fishing is just a matter of throwing down a line or a net and hauling up a fish? A good fisherman knows his gear, his boats, his machinery, the best roots to use when making lobster traps. He knows how to sniff the air and observe the sky for signs of unforecasted winds and fogs. He knows his bait, his times of day, his sea bottom, the choices of where to go and how soon. A talented fisherman knows all these things and much more. And—in spite of the wrenching cold, the disappointments, the fluky comings and goings of the fish population—he loves what he is doing with his life. I know this to be true. I spent half my boyhood tagging along with any local fishermen who'd put up with me—on their Cape Island boats, their Tancooks, or just in their dories.

No one on Bay Street can describe to you the feeling of setting out through a band of sunrise on the water, trailing five seine boats, a faint wind rising. Or the serenity that fills your chest as you strike out to sea, aimed at the dead centre of the horizon, focused on Africa. That's what I'd longed and hoped for from the time I was five years old. At sixteen, it was still my dream.

The exam results came in, just four days before my seventeenth birthday. I stood at the mailbox, holding my marks: the highest in grade twelve for the whole of the county. And more. The biggest university scholarship for that region, puffed out with some subsistence money donated by a local boy who'd made good on Wall Street. I took all of it and laid it on the kitchen table.

"I don't want it" is all I said.

My father and mother looked at the marks, read the letter, raised their eyes, and looked at me. My mother had her mask on. Not my father.

"What in blazing hell do you mean—you don't *want* it?"

"I don't want to go to college. I want to stay here. I want to be a fisherman. The best one around. It's what I've always wanted, ever since I laid eyes on a boat."

My father stood up. He was skinny, but he looked big that day. With one abrupt gesture, he swept everything off the kitchen table onto the floor—four coffee mugs, *The Daily News*, cutlery, Ma's books, a pot with a geranium in it, a loaded ashtray.

"You want to be a fisherman!" he shouted. "Us with no gear, no wharf, no shed, no launch. Not even a decent-size boat. No, young fella! You turn down that offer and you got but one route to take. Me, I'll teach you how to do it, because I'm the best gutter in the plant."

He paused for a breath. Then again: "*No,* dammit! You just pitch out your fancy dreams and grab that scholarship, because I'm sure not gonna keep you here any longer come fall. Not if you can make money with that fool book-learning that your prissy ma seems to have passed along with her mother's milk." He smashed his fist down on the empty table and kicked his way out the back door.

∽

Ma died when I was twenty-four, just one week before I received my M.B.A. from the University of Toronto. I'd picked up two other degrees on the way, and had sailed through university with accolades and scholarships. There I was, half an orphan, embarking on a life of prosperity and maladjustment, cut off by my past and my present from my original dream.

I skipped graduation and flew home for the funeral. I stayed three weeks. Pa was silent and shrunken-looking, although he was only fifty-five. He sat around a lot, guzzling beer, going through two packs of cigarettes a day. The only kid left at home was Amery, and he looked as though he'd like nothing better than to jump ship. Thin and fidgety, he'd startle if you so much as snapped your fingers. He was working in the plant, too. Gutting.

"Thinkin' o' closin' down the plant," said Pa, one day. "No fish worth a darn. Most o' the time, anyways. Foreign vessels scoopin' 'em all up before they has a chance to spawn."

He didn't say this angrily. He said it wearily, as though he had nothing but lukewarm water flowing through his veins. And no blood transfusion in sight.

The day I left, I waited until Amery and Pa had departed for work. Then I went out and sat on the wood-pile. The offshore wind was blowing strong and dry, and the gulls were coasting around in the sky, wings spread, barely twitching. The sun was well up, casting a wide path over the ruffled water. While I watched, a Cape Islander crossed the path, low in the water with a big catch of mackerel. In the distance, the horizon stretched taut and firm, broken by the leaping waves of the four reefs.

I searched in vain for Africa. Apparently it wasn't there anymore.

Confusion

Clara Adams is sitting in church—her *father's* church—thinking about how simple her life used to be. You woke up in the morning and went to school, unless it happened to be a weekend or summertime, in which case you went out to play. You loved both of your parents. You idolized your big brother, Mark, and thought Joanie, your younger sister, was a pest. You said your prayers before you went to bed, and you went to church, absolutely without fail, every Sunday. You believed everything your father said about God, Jesus, sin, resisting temptation, angels, heaven.

Clara sighs so loudly that her mother digs her in the ribs with her elbow. Her father, tall and handsome in an odd, unorthodox way (his nose is a bit too long, and his mouth too thin), is in the middle of one of his endless

prayers. Clara can see that Mr. Johnson—one pew over—
is fast asleep, his head wagging on his neck, his chin
bumping his chest. She feels a fierce pleasure in this, and
hopes that her father is noticing him. But of course he's
not. His eyes are tight shut, and his face is lifted far
above the congregation—as though he knew that if he
opened them, he'd see a flock of angels perched on the
chandelier.

Her father is listing, in unnecessary detail, the reasons
for an impassioned and generous worship of God.
Impassioned because you absolutely must feel and believe
everything intensely—like the *fact* that God is all-wise, all-
knowing, all-good. Generous, Clara realizes (because she
has heard versions of this prayer a thousand times), means
that, without a single backward glance, you give your
time and your labours to those who are less fortunate, and
that you put a whole lot of money on the collection plate
when it comes winging around during the next hymn.

But Clara is bored with all of this. I've gone to church
one day too many, she thinks, and I'm no longer entirely
sure that God *is* all that wise, that knowledgeable, that
good. Surely a wise God wouldn't leave those street
people out there on the sidewalk when it's ten below zero.
And what about wars? What's the good of being all-
knowing if you don't stop some of the bad stuff you're so
knowledgeable about? And how could an all-good God
let that little Corkum kid get killed last week on the cross-
walk? If He's so all-wise and all-good, why doesn't He
ever *explain* anything?

Clara is eighteen years old. She's old enough to leave home without consent, drink alcohol in bars, and join the army. So this isn't the first time she's had these thoughts. And she knows why she's having a replay of them this morning. It's because of last night. Clara bows her head and shuts her eyes.

She knew the minute she saw him standing there on the stoop that he was the mystery man that she'd been waiting for—and suspecting might never appear. Rachel Schneider, Clara's best friend ever since kindergarten, started falling in love in grade *five*. And six or seven more times before she was out of junior high. Not Clara. But that was more or less okay. She knew it would happen in high school.

She remembered when Arthur Hudson arrived in their grade ten classroom, straight out of Ontario's biggest city—Toronto, home of the Blue Jays and the CN Tower, capital of Canada's richest province, centre of everything musical, cultural, sinful, celebrated, sophisticated, *right*. And there he was—knowing full well that he was a city mouse among a roomful of country mice—athletic, proud, at ease. Almost every girl in the class was instantly in love with him. And Clara? No. She didn't let it happen. She was too busy assessing his worth and finding him deficient. Deciding he was conceited, overconfident, out for number one.

It was the same story in grade eleven, when she found herself in Chuck O'Brien's home room. *Six girls* in the class adored him. But not Clara. She certainly liked him.

But where were the fireworks and sparks that she'd read about? Why wasn't she feeling faint or dizzy? Why did her heart continue its steady regular beat?

Clara glances at her mother, whose concentration never seems to flag. Her father is listing sins at the moment and asking the congregation to confess their own. To regret their greed, lust, anger, lack of faith, self-centredness, procrastination, laziness. Why isn't her mother jumping off the pew and shouting, "You've got some of those sins yourself, fella. It's not just *us*." Clara doesn't know how her mom has endured—for twenty-five years!—hearing all those virtuous exhortations from someone she has watched being lazy, angry, self-centred. Not all that *often*—but still . . . Clara closes her eyes so that she can take another hard look at last evening.

She'd arrived home late after basketball practice. It was April 9 and the final playoffs were only a week away. You missed a practice at your peril. Being late for dinner just wasn't an issue. So when the doorbell rang, she had just arrived home. Her face and hands were dirty; she was sweaty and smelly; her hair (black, curly, and unmanageable at the best of times) was standing out from her head like a witch's halo. She was panting from running all the way from school, knowing they had a guest for supper.

There he was at the doorway, smiling. He was very thin, with a lot of yellow hair, a broad nose, huge hands. She took in all of this before either of them spoke a word. Although he was standing still, she could tell he was loose-jointed and maybe uncoordinated. He'd probably trip on thresholds and bump into doors. But he didn't have that paralyzing shyness she so detested. Or, in fact, the conceit, which she hated even worse. She looked at him and knew he was perfect. All the predictable things happened. Her knees (so ready for any manoeuvre on the basketball floor) were threatening to collapse from under her. Her hands flew to her unruly hair, patting down its wildness. Her breath was deserting her, her heart pounding, although she had the best recovery rate on the basketball team.

As it appeared that she was incapable of speech, he spoke first.

"Hi," he said, and whatever ambivalence she might have felt collapsed under the spell of his voice. The depth of it! All in that one "Hi." But then he said, "Is this still the Adams house? If so, I'm here for dinner. I'm Pete Vincent."

Clara, who had heretofore been so many of the things she abhorred—over confident, proud, critical—now lapsed into the paralysis of shyness that she had also found so trying in other people.

"Come in," she said, backing up, bumping into the hall table, coughing to cover up her embarrassment. Then Clara—old enough for marriage, taverns, the armed forces, motherhood—left him standing there in the hall, and fled to the kitchen to find her mother. There she was, stirring something at the stove, a reassuring sight.

"Mom," she said, voice faint, "someone called Pete Vincent is here. He says he came for supper. Can you look after him? I need a shower."

Her mother sounded brisk. "Yes," she said. "You certainly do. But you, the dinner, and Pete Vincent are all late, and if we don't start dinner *this minute,* it'll start tasting like sawdust."

"But—" Clara was running her fingers frantically through her hair.

"I know," said her mother, glancing at her as she started draining the vegetables. "Pretty awful. But it's only Pete. He's been here before when you were out. He's just a Dal student who thinks he might want to become a United Church minister. He likes to talk things out with your dad. He won't mind all that sweat. I hear your father out there talking to him."

Dinner was torture. Mark, Clara's erstwhile idol, was doing his boredom thing. He was probably Pete's age, but that's where the similarity ended. He was an engineering student, and no way was he going to get involved in a discussion about theology. Clara had never noticed before how rude he could be. Joanie kept interrupting the conversation to discuss various aspects of her day in grade nine. Her father was clearly annoyed; her mother was apparently oblivious to all the cross-currents; but Pete was patient, even asking Joanie some questions about her school. When he said to Clara, "I hear you're an avid basketball player," she got a piece of lettuce caught in her throat and had a coughing fit. She wished profoundly that she could disappear like a whiff of smoke.

But when Pete went home (early, because he had an exam on Monday) she offered to do the dishes alone, just so she could think without being disturbed by Joanie's yackety-yack or Mark's silence. Either one would be unbearable right now. Later, she lay on her bed and did replays of everything that was good in the evening—Pete's voice, his smile, his giant bony hands *(touch me, touch me)*, his courtesy.

And now she's in church.

And what she's thinking is: *I'm eighteen years old, and I've just fallen in love for the first time. I can't believe anyone could be so backward, so emotionally retarded. Ginny Halliday is getting married this July; she's still only seventeen and she's not even pregnant. And when the delayed miracle finally decided to happen to me, why did it have to be with Pete Vincent? Someone who wants to be a clergyman, for God's sake. Someone who must have got all that religion stuff worked out donkey's years ago. Someone who wouldn't touch me with even the tip of his index finger if he knew about the confusion roiling around in my head. I can't stand the way Dad is so judgmental, but I spend half my own waking hours criticizing God. I don't like shy, wimpy women, but last night when Pete came to dinner, I got so seized up with bashfulness that I couldn't get my tongue untangled from my teeth. What's wrong with me?*

Mrs. Adams nudges Clara in the ribs again. The interminable prayer is apparently over, and everyone is fumbling around in pockets and purses for collection money. The organ is about to rev up for the offertory hymn, and people are shuffling to their feet.

Clara looks around the church, seeing familiar faces: old Mrs. Henry, who still thinks you should wear a hat to church (mauve straw, with purple violets); Mr. Johnson, who has finally shuddered into wakefulness; Miss Sullivan, Clara's teacher in grade four, who had all the compassion of a serial killer when any of the kids stepped out of line; Mr. Rothsay, who ever since Clara can remember has kept jelly beans in his pocket to hand out to the kids; Mrs. Houston, who brought them all those casseroles when Mrs. Adams was down with the flu this past winter; Dr. and Mrs. Cameron, who made such a stinking fuss about the colour chosen for the back wall of the vestibule, when the painters (at no cost) spruced up the church last fall.

And then she sees him—because he's so tall—standing way over on the other side of the nave. He's singing lustily and looks like he's enjoying himself. Clara's chest once again feels like a hollow cave, and when she turns over the page of the hymn book, she sees that her hand is shaking. She frowns. This is ridiculous. She's used to feeling so sure of herself.

Now they're all sitting down, making small rustling sounds as they adjust themselves into comfortable positions. The sermon is next. Miss Sullivan is sitting up very straight, looking so absolutely confident of God's approval. How lovely, thinks Clara, to be perpetually sure of everything. But she doesn't really think it's lovely. She thinks it's disgusting.

Clara's father's sermon is on the subject of humility. *A tailor-made subject for Miss Sullivan,* thinks Clara, *and maybe for me. And also for him—for Dad. Anyone who spends every Sunday and a lot of weekdays telling people that they ought to be good, honest, kind, patient, generous, unprejudiced, energetic, and industrious can't be very humble himself.* She dares to glance over to the right to grab a quick look at Pete. He's listening avidly. He obviously thinks her father is some kind of guru, an acceptable substitute for the real thing—for God, to be exact. *Wait till he discovers that the Reverend Hugh Adams is bigoted about rock music, given to road rage when other drivers tailgate or pass on a yellow line, lazier than a slug on Mondays, and often petulant if you're even thirty seconds late. He was probably irritated as hell last night when Pete was fifteen minutes late for supper, but he's not going to let any of those little sins be visible in front of a potential theological student.*

Clara is pleased that Pete likes her father so much. She also hates it. If Pete likes him, he'll come often to his house—to *her* house. He'll maybe think of what a wonderful father-in-law he'd be. But she hates it, because Pete obviously thinks her dad is perfect, and he isn't. Just as she thinks Pete is perfect. Who just possibly may not be any such thing.

As she listens to the sermon, Clara is already married. That's Pete up there, his unruly blond hair severely slicked back, his beautiful voice informing his adoring flock about the necessity for humility. They're believing every word he says, and at least seven of the young unmarried women in the congregation are deeply in love with him. And some of the elderly spinsters, too.

While Pete continues his sermon—with a special mention of the sin of anger—she's remembering the way he scolded the twins last night (their third and fourth children) and how high and mighty he sounded. She's finding it difficult to sit here and listen to him urge people to be perfect when he isn't perfect himself. But she's the minister's wife, so she has to smile and smile, pretending a whole lot of things that she doesn't feel.

Clara is back in her own skin now, and it's time for the closing hymn. She loves hymns, has always loved them. She enjoys getting swept along by the simple melodies, by the thundering organ, by the sound of so many voices singing together. And if the words of the hymn somehow or other hit the nail on the head, she can begin to feel eager to change herself into a nicer—and less confused—person. She can imagine herself saying, "Hi, God! I know you're there, even if I don't always recognize you."

Clara smiles, and looks over at Pete. Incredibly, he's watching her, and his wide mouth is breaking into a grin. She feels herself red and hot, but full of an identifiable joy. She thinks about Rachel Schneider, who has been in love so often, and with such fanfare. Lucky, lucky Rachel. But this, of course, is different, better. Rachel's loves come and go; they can't possibly reach the intensity of what Clara is feeling for Pete. Besides, Clara knows that this love is permanent. She wishes he didn't want to be a minister. Why couldn't he be an architect or a farmer or someone linked less openly to sin and virtue? Right now, she's mostly wishing that she could be more like her mother, for whom things seem to be so . . . *straightforward.*

As Clara and Mrs. Adams wash the dishes together later that day, Clara asks, "Do you ever think you'd like to be something besides a minister's wife?"

Her mother is busy drying a plate, but she pauses and holds it close to her chest. "Yes," she says.

Clara is amazed. "Why?"

"I'd like to be someone who wasn't expected to be so visibly well-behaved all the time. I'd like to be able to kick down a door occasionally without the sky falling."

Clara is wondering why it's taken her eighteen years to discover all this.

"What about sermons? Does it bother you to hear Dad telling everyone to control their anger, when you know he blew up at Mark last night for losing the car keys?"

Mrs. Adams laughs. "Oh, sure," she says. "Especially if he's sounding too *holy* about it. But I can't expect him to be perfect. He's not God, you know. And fortunately he realizes it. He's aware of his short fuse, and he's working on it." She laughs again. "He's been working on it for twenty-five years."

Clara feels she may as well try the really hard one.

"What about God?"

"Well, what about Him?"

"Why did He make such an imperfect world? All that cruelty and starvation and greed. All those wars. All the sorrow. Drownings. Plane crashes. Autism. Cerebral palsy. Cancer. And what about *death*? Why does He have to *do* all that awful stuff?"

Mrs. Adams is sitting down on a kitchen chair by now. She's completely stopped drying dishes, and they're piling up in the drainer.

"Years ago," she says, "I knew an elderly and feisty nun. I can remember her saying, 'Poor God. People blame Him for everything.' I can't answer your question. I'm sure your father can't, either. It's impossible to explain all those tragedies and horrors. And very hard to accept them. I'm sure there must be days when even the pope has long, hard moments of doubt."

"*Nobody* can explain it?"

They're both sitting at the kitchen table now, drinking leftover coffee, the dishes forgotten. Mrs. Adams is stirring and stirring her coffee.

"People try, of course," she says. "But I feel they always fail. It's too big a question for mere people to answer. Probably there's a big plan unfolding somewhere, somehow. But we can't *prove* it in the usual ways." She pauses. "Why haven't you asked your dad about all these things? He's quite a guy, you know. He thinks a lot and knows a lot and struggles a lot. Besides, he's been around for eighteen of your eighteen years, and it's sort of his territory."

"I was afraid he'd be shocked by my teetering faith."

Mrs. Adams laughs again. "He knows all about teetering faith. It's a malady he suffers from himself. Most people do." She pauses and looks hard at Clara. "Including Pete Vincent."

Clara feels a wave of relief, embarrassment, amusement, and she blushes a deep, uneasy red. Relief that he doesn't think he's perfect. Embarrassment and amusement because her mother seems to be a mindreader.

"How did you figure all that out?"

Her mother chuckles.

"I never before heard you ask to take a shower when you were late for dinner. Your coordination went a little crazy. You kept patting your hair. You choked on the salad. I'm not stupid. I know the signs."

Mother and daughter grin at one another. "How'll I know if it's the real thing?" says Clara.

"You won't. You kind of have to accept your responses and tally up a lot of data. And then take a huge leap of faith. Just like with the other things we've been talking about. Also," and here her mother laughs again, "I wouldn't start planning your whole married life on the basis of one meeting."

But of course Clara is doing exactly that. She's thinking about her responses and trusting them absolutely. She hasn't any data at all to tally up, but she'll make sure that her eyes and ears are ready to absorb any that materialize. And she's happy to think that both the pope and her father have moments of doubt.

As for Clara, she figures it may take her a lifetime to get that God stuff sorted out. But at least she's not as *mad* at Him as she usually is. Or at her father, for that matter. "Give them a break," she mutters to herself. Apparently no one is perfect, which is certainly a relief. If Pete becomes a minister, maybe he actually *will* practise what he preaches, although living in the same house with all that undiluted virtue could be quite a strain. Clara turns over on her stomach and grins into the pillow. *What a tangled mess of confusion I am. But who cares? Mom said that Pete was coming to dinner on Tuesday night. I'll process the data and register my responses. That'll be enough to keep me busy. I think it's all I can handle right now. I'll leave the universe for another time.*

Crybaby

It's not as though I was an unusual infant. I acted pretty much like any other baby boy I've ever heard of. I cried when I was hungry, wet, lonely. I don't remember any of that, of course. But my mother told me about it. She said I did a lot of howling. She told me how I kept her awake at night, deprived her of sleep, filled her with pointless anxieties. She wondered if there was something wrong with me. After all, it looked like a pretty cushy life to her—just lying in that bassinet or in my playpen, surrounded by woolly toys, watching the Donald Duck mobile. Whereas she had to hang my wet clothes out on the line in the frigid winter weather, because she had no dryer. She was forced to heat and sterilize bottles, because she certainly wasn't going to strangle her other schedules by being confined to breast feeding. It was depressing enough, she said, to contemplate what childbearing had done to her figure. And of course the other part of her life had to go on against the background music of that constant wailing. Shopping and cooking and cleaning didn't just grind to a halt because there was a baby in the house. No siree. And there were diapers—cloth ones—to be scraped, soaked, washed, disinfected. She made certain that toilet training took place very early in my life. Her peers—struggling with potties and bribes and training pants and midnight accidents—marvelled at her. How could she possibly have managed to train me so early? But over the years I've heard her say a hundred times, "It can be done. Anyone can do it. People just don't try hard enough." She didn't have any more children. I was an only child.

Trying hard enough became what the three of us who lived in that house were supposed to aim for. Of course, my mother had the philosophy down cold, long before I learned how to speak or listen or think coherently. My father was already halfway there. He was an ambitious but unsuccessful man who wanted everything to go his way—or *come* his way—including the top positions in the large bottling plant he worked for. Since his chosen method for reaching the top was through bluster and bulldozing, it's not surprising that he stayed pretty close to the bottom rung of the corporate ladder. Naturally, this state of affairs added frustration and a pervading sense of injustice to his already aggressive nature. The mixture wasn't beneficial to any of us.

My memory goes back pretty far, and I can remember a lot of things about when I was three. Because I was toilet-trained, I could be shipped out to a playschool as soon as I was two. In those times, day care facilities were almost non-existent, but if you looked hard enough you could find unlicensed ones. And of course my mother looked hard. I can't remember entering this so-called school, but I've been informed many times that I cried in that place for five straight days. But by the age of three I was a conformist. I played in the sandbox, enjoyed both dolls and trucks, struggled with the puzzles, ate my arrow-root cookies at ten A.M., painted messy pictures. I liked nursery school, and I can remember the liking of it. It was more peaceful than my home.

At 23 Withrow Street, which is where we lived, my mother's rules were clear. I was to stay as clean as possible, make as little noise as I could, and keep out of her way. Crying was noise, so I learned very early that a skinned knee or a nasty friend or a nightmare was not sufficient cause for tears. They weren't tragic enough to qualify as roadblocks to her rigid agendas. A crying child could stretch an hour of meal preparation to an hour and a quarter. Grocery shopping wasn't as efficient and quick if I yelled when a can of Campbell's tomato soup (large size) fell on my toe. And I knew what not to do if she was engrossed in watching her favourite TV show. Still, in the very rare moments when my mother wasn't engaged in doing anything specific or planned, I might feel at liberty to cry. I remember her comforting me once or twice with hugs. I can recall those times, even now, at the age of forty. The feeling was warm, like the hot water bottle she used for her aching back. It was soft, like the small yellow blanket that I hugged at bedtime. It was also safe, in the way a best friend provides you with social safety.

When I was eight, my father gave me a dog. He didn't buy him, that's for sure. No one would be selling a dog that was so visibly a misfit, so clearly a mongrel. He was a mixture of a dozen breeds. His nose was blunt when it should have been sharp. His long hair was destined to be forever muddy, because it was too close to every puddle he waded through. Besides, he loved to roll in things—in piles of crisp leaves, in street gutters, in my mother's vegetable garden. His tail was too bushy, his legs were too short. But his eyes were large and eloquent; they told me without question that he adored me. And I loved him with a passion that even now can bring a lump to my throat. I called him Sherlock. I'd heard the name and liked it. It suited him, I felt.

"Every boy should have a dog," my father had announced on the day he brought him home, without, I might add, having consulted my mother. I cannot even attempt to describe my extravagant joy when that shaggy mutt emerged from the box my father had placed upon the floor. Nothing else mattered. My mother's coldness and my father's furies faded into the background of a life that was instantly dominated by Sherlock.

Sherlock—in the eyes of my mother, and often in the eyes of my father (who hadn't thought to look beyond the experiences of getting and giving)—knew how to do everything wrong. He barked too much, irritating the neighbours, who complained. But he wagged his tail at strangers and was useless as a watchdog. After rolling in the leaves, he would come in and deposit them all over my mother's clean house. He scratched at the door at six A.M., waking everyone up—as well as removing a significant amount of cream-coloured paint. My mother's prized slip-covers grew dingy, were covered with hairs, even developed a few little rips that were hard to mend. If I had looked carefully, I would have seen more clearly the expression on Mom's face as she coped with all those traumas.

But I wasn't looking carefully. Sherlock and I took off every afternoon after school, sometimes with my best friend, Rolly. More often we were alone. We raced up and down the hills of the old Gorsebrook golf course. We ran all over both sides of Spring Garden Road and terrorized old ladies. We rolled down Citadel Hill together, and locked ourselves into a passionate embrace at the bottom. I told him my thoughts, and shared with him my sorrow and fears and reined-in anger. I knew we were going to be together and happy forever.

Forever lasted about six months, which I now see was quite a long time for my mother to put up with something she didn't like or approve of. But Dad had given me the dog, and she was afraid of her husband.

There was an executive position open at the bottling plant. Mr. Jamieson had died of a sudden heart attack, leaving the job vacant. My father wanted it with an intensity that was almost scary. Even I—busy with school, with kick-the-can, with Rolly, with Sherlock—could see that. Noisily he pursued that job, telling his supervisor how suited he was for it, how clever, how indispensable. He collared the president of the company on Barrington Street and listed his brownie points, his talents, his worthiness. He told of all those things at the supper table over his Campbell's tomato soup. My mother looked at him, her face blank. She knew he was going about it all wrong; she knew that trying hard has to be coupled with some sort of wiliness. But she said nothing. He'd hit her once after he'd had a bad day, and he was a big man.

He didn't get the position. A man from Truro was brought in to fill the space, and my father stayed exactly where he was, in the dead-end job he would occupy until he retired with his gold watch at the age of sixty—five years early—because of pathological stress and chronic high blood pressure.

The day my father found out about the Truro man was a rainy fall day, full of wind. He entered the house late for supper, straight from the Seahorse Tavern, red in the face, eyes like black stones. My mother looked angry at first (the fish cakes were dried up, the peas wrinkled), but her expression changed to one of alarm. He told us. He yelled it all out, cursing the Truro man, the stupidity of the company, the injustices of the entire planet. The door blew open and Sherlock bounded in, fresh from the nearest mud puddle, wet leaves clinging to his coat, barking. He jumped up at my father, full of a joyous welcome, spraying him with mud, with leaves, with doggy smell.

My dad didn't pause. He kicked Sherlock clear across the room—so hard that you could hear the impact of his shoe—shouting, "If someone doesn't get rid of that dirty damn dog, I'm gonna take my twenty-two and shoot him!" My mother smiled quietly in the middle of the chaos. "You're absolutely right, Gerald," she said soothingly. "There's not an inch of this house that he hasn't scratched or ripped or soiled. I've been wondering myself how long I could stand it."

Sherlock was crouched in the corner, whimpering. I was sure he was hurt, and I was aching to help him, but I was afraid to move. I felt that if I approached him, I might add to the rage that was already threatening his very existence. The fact that I failed to comfort him was to haunt me off and on until I was a grown man.

I didn't see it happen. When I returned from school the next day, Sherlock simply was not there. To this day, I don't know what they did with him. I was afraid to ask, lest the answer destroy me with its awfulness.

But I cried. I cried and cried. I couldn't stop. There was only one more day left before the weekend, so they kept me home and sent a note to the teacher, saying I had stomach flu. Sometimes I would stop for awhile, but not for long. Like a cyclical thunderstorm, waves of grief would return to throw me into new fits of crying. "Stop it!" my father yelled on Friday night. "*Just stop it!*" Guilt—and possibly even remorse—may have been piled on top of his feelings of defeat, betrayal, and rage. I doubt if he was angry at just the bottling company or the dog anymore—or me. He was angry at the whole world.

On Saturday morning, faced with my noisy crying again, he roared, "How long do we have to listen to this?" and sent me to my room. I stayed in there all day. My mother brought up a tray with my favourite sandwich and a chocolate-covered cookie. I ate none of it. My crying would cease for a time, and then start up again. The recurring storm was still rampaging. At five o'clock, my father noisily mounted the stairs and opened my door.

"Stop your damn crying, you stupid little crybaby," he said. He spoke quietly, through his teeth, his mouth almost closed. I was howling full out as he spoke, but I saw him and heard him. The quietness of his voice deceived me. Then he crossed the room and hit me across the side of my face with the back of his hand—the hand on which he wore his signet ring.

I stopped crying as swiftly and absolutely as if I had been shot in the head. I could feel something snap in me, with an almost audible click. I stared at my father as he left the room, slamming the door behind him. I remember my mother coming up and wiping the blood off my face, bathing it in warm water. I stayed home from school for a week and a half, until my face looked almost normal again. It was a very bad case of the flu, my mother explained to the teacher.

～

I passed through my years of childhood and youth with the usual miseries that afflict the young: accidents, broken friendships, family battles, a broken bone or two, grave disappointments, injustices. But I never cried once during all that time. When grief or hurt would take hold and tears threaten, I would feel a tightness in my chest and throat like a band of steel, and I would remain dry-eyed and brittle.

Time passed. I graduated from high school with high marks in English and history, and then left university five years later, with a master's degree (which, my father pointed out, could lead to nothing except unemployment). I financed my schooling myself, through an array of part-time jobs—gardener, construction worker, plumber's helper, college janitor, essay marker, pizza cook, to name but a few. I lived at home during all of those years. My M.A. was a good one, and I was taken on as a lecturer at St. Mary's University, in spite of my lack of a Ph.D.

So my father had been wrong. There I was, twenty-five years old, with a job that pleased me and—at last—an apartment of my own in North Halifax, from which I travelled each day to the university on a second-hand bicycle. I was as happy as a person can be who is socially inept, emotionally fettered, and philosophically naïve. I had always considered myself to be a misfit, and I clung to that notion.

But—wonder of wonders—the students liked me and responded well to my teaching. I discovered that I had a sense of humour, and unearthed a lot of things to laugh about. Best of all, at the age of twenty-six, I met a kind and lively young woman called Shelagh, who possessed none of my mother's rigid agendas or my father's twitchy nervous system. It was like setting my boat on a calm, translucent lake, after a long journey over a grey and turbulent sea. I loved her literally more than my own life, but my own life was stunted, and there was a quality to my loving that was constrained and troubled. She wanted very badly to have a baby, but I kept procrastinating, dreaming up reasons why this wasn't a good time in history to bring a child into the world. Everyone was agitating about pollution and overpopulation and nuclear weapons. But those weren't my real reasons. Sometimes I could feel an unreasonable anger rising in myself, and I was afraid that I'd be an abusive father. I told all of this to Shelagh. "You're crazy," she said. "I've never met a man so gentle and just." But she didn't know what was going on in my head, or about the band of steel that kept my emotions in check.

We didn't find the dog. The dog found us. He came to the back door one Thursday evening, looking thin and hungry. We fed him—that night and throughout the weekend. He didn't look one bit like Sherlock, but he was clearly a dog with no pedigree of any kind, so I felt a kinship.

We called him Watson, after the friend and confidante of Sherlock Holmes. Ours was a case of instant reciprocal love. We advertised his discovery in both city newspapers, and prayed that no one would respond to our ad. He was small and nondescript, with a big appetite and a lot of energy. He loved both of us, and greeted our arrival home at the end of each day as though we'd been absent for a month, probably in a war zone. His stubby little tail was in constant motion. He trembled all over with delight when we offered food, balls, sticks, walks, swims, or just words of praise. No one claimed him. He became ours; it was a three-way love affair.

We took Watson for long walks along the shore path at Point Pleasant Park. At Hubbards Beach he raced in and out of the sea like some sort of water animal. I ran with him on Citadel Hill, and hoped that Sherlock wouldn't mind that I was enjoying it so much. He slept on our bed, snuggled up to Shelagh's knees one night, to mine the next. With diplomatic sensitivity, he treated us with equal amounts of affection. We were a happy family. Shelagh stopped nagging me about the baby.

One day in early June, about two years after we adopted Watson, we took him to Crescent Beach for a long run. He loved it, and ran up and down the hard-packed sand, yelping with joy. It was a bright but chilly day, and the two and a half miles of beach were deserted. Suddenly a car appeared from the main road and bumped onto the beach. Cars often drive on the beach in off-seasons, and June in Nova Scotia is not high summer. This one contained a load of noisy young people, singing, shouting, tossing beer bottles out the windows. We called Watson to come back to us, but he was having too good a time to listen. He was about a quarter of a mile down the beach, so far away that we could hardly make out his wagging tail. The car was racing in that direction, weaving crazily across the sand. After it passed the spot where he was, we could see no movement—just a small dark form on the ground.

Shelagh was frozen to the spot on which she stood, but I ran down the beach and reached him, just as the car made its return journey, its occupants singing, laughing. Watson opened his eyes for maybe one second, and then closed them. His tail gave one last jerk. I placed my hand on his body to feel for pulse or breathing, but I knew that he was dead. I picked him up and, carried him back to Shelagh, the steel band tight around my throat and chest. I laid him carefully on our blanket on the sand, and hugged Shelagh close to me for a long time. Then, propelled by who knows what impulse, I released her, and raced across the sand again as fast as I could go. I may have run for half a mile. Then I stopped. I knew I was completely alone. I raised my fists in the air and screamed to the sky, screamed and screamed until my voice cracked and hurt. Then I dropped to my knees, and I could feel rusty wheels turning inside me. I started to cry, at first slowly, quietly, with tears barely squeezing out of my eyes. Then I gathered force and volume, and cried in loud racking sobs that shook my body. I cried for Watson and for Sherlock, and for every remembered grief and rage that I had ever felt. No child could have cried more loudly or more nakedly than I did that day.

When I finally stopped, I felt very still. I looked out at the wide expanse of sea and recognized that something had changed. What was it? *The band of steel was gone.* About fifty feet away, I could see Shelagh standing, keeping distance between us, knowing she should let this thing happen. When I beckoned for her to come, she ran to me, and we held one another until the rising tide nearly reached us.

We walked through the water's edge back to our picnic spot. "I've been thinking," I said, when I was finally able to speak, "about that baby of ours. Now seems a good time. What do you think?" She looked up at me, and there were still one or two tears sliding down her face. But she smiled and nodded.

We wrapped Watson up in our best beach towel and put him on the back seat of our car, along with all the blankets and Thermos bottles and food containers. Then we put on our sneakers, climbed into the car, and headed for home.

Mr. Manuel Jenkins

I remember well the day he came. It was autumn, which starts early in Nova Scotia and is always for me a time of joy and bitterness. The onset of winter is hard to accept after a summer that is so short and a fall that is so brilliantly beautiful. And in some parts of the province, winter can seem as forever as dying. As early as the second week in August, my mother would say, "I feel fall in the air," and my heart would lurch a little.

It was late September, and some of the low-lying bushes were already scarlet against the black of the evergreen forest. Dried flowers waved stiffly against the blue of the bay, but the gulls were acting as though nothing had changed, as though sailing above on the wind currents were enough for them, now and for always.

It had been a bad day for me, and the splendour of the

afternoon rebuked me. Beauty can be an aching thing when you are unhappy, and I have always welcomed fog and rain—or better still, a storm—when I am sad. Otherwise, I can feel a pull back to balance; and misery, for me, has always been half in love with itself.

The reasons for my depression were not dramatic. No one had died; the house had not burned down; I hadn't failed a test in school or lost a boyfriend. But I was fifteen, a time of limbo for me, and a period of trigger-happy nerves. Neither child nor woman, I wanted to be both and sometimes neither. For one thing, I longed to adore my mother again; but she irritated me almost beyond endurance, with her obsession with food and cleanliness and good behaviour—and with her refusal to listen to what I was or was not saying. I wanted her to see right into my head and heart and to congratulate me on their contents. Instead, she ignored or misconstrued or *misdirected* even the things I said aloud. For instance, that morning I had said to her, "Mom, it's such a divine day. I'm going to take the boat out to Crab Island and just sit on a rock and be me all day long."

To which she replied, "You can be you right here in the kitchen this very minute and help me defrost the fridge." Which I did. After that she said, "What's the use of going out to Crab Island all by yourself? You could at least take Sarah with you. She's been galumphing around the house and driving me crazy. If you go alone, she won't even have the boat to play in." And where did that leave me? Either I stayed home and nursed the hot ball of resentment that inhabited my stomach almost constantly of late; or I went to the island with Sarah, age twelve, whose main characteristic was never shutting up for one second, and who always wanted to be *doing* something—like *exploring*, or *skipping stones*, or writing X's and O's on the granite cliff with rocks—*scrape, scrape, scrape*—when I'd be wanting to soak up the stillness. I opted for home and the hot ball of resentment.

My mom was the big boss in our home. Do this, do that, and we all did it. Jump! and we jumped. Even my dad jumped. He had a slow and kindly heart, unending patience, and a warm smile. That had been enough for me for years and years. But suddenly this year it wasn't. I wanted him to look my mother in the eye and say, "I live here, too. I caught that fish you're frying in the pan. If I want to go hunting this afternoon, I'll go. And you can just stop ordering me around like I was in kindergarten." But that morning he'd spoken to her as she was thunking down the rolling pin on the cookie dough at the kitchen table. "Gert," he said slowly, tentatively, as though he already anticipated her answer, "I thought maybe I'd go over to Barrington this afternoon and see old Sam Hiltz. Haven't had a visit with him for near two years. I'm kind of tuckered out. Feel like I could sort of use a day off."

"We could all use a day off," she said tartly, no softness in her anywhere. "If women ever took a day off, their families would starve to death in twenty-four hours. And by the time they got back, they'd have to spend longer than their day off cleaning up the bathroom and the kitchen." She delivered to him a piercing look. "Why, I can go shopping in Shelburne for two hours, and come back to find the kitchen sink looking like the washbasin at the drive-in." She stopped attacking the dough and started forming shapes with the cookie-cutter. No diamonds or hearts on that pan, ever. Or chickens or gingerbread men. All her cookies were round. "And do you think these cookies drop out of the sky?" she went on. "Chocolate chips all firmly in place? Or that an angel flies down and deposits your clean laundry on the bed each Monday evening? No siree. I need that car this afternoon to pick up a parcel at Sears. Old Sam can wait till the next time you feel a holiday coming over you. And if you've got that little to do, how about bringing in some water. Or wood. Or lettuce from the garden. Or *something*."

I wanted to take the pans of round cookies, all the same size, all placed exactly one half-inch from each other, and throw them through the window. I imagined the crash as they hit the window, visualized the little slivers of glass protruding from the dough. And I wanted to yell at my sweet and silent father, *Do* something! *Answer* her! Say, It's my car. I paid for it. Go to Sears *tomorrow*. Old Sam is ninety-two years old and sick, and he might die this afternoon.

Or he could have said, To hell with all that food! Curses on your stupid cookies! We're all overweight in this family, all six of us. And we don't need to be that *clean*. Even without any plumbing, some people live to be 110 years old. Sit down. Fold your hands. Take the time to talk to us a spell. Or better still, to listen.

But no. Off he went, down to the government wharf to discuss the day's catch with his friends.

And outside the kitchen, the soft gold September sun shed radiance upon the face of the sea. The sky was cloudless and almost as blue as the bay. Such beauty was beckoning, and not one of us could see it.

And then he came. Straight up to the front door, where no one ever came. Knocking three times, he waited, hat in hand, and I opened the door.

The loveliness of the day had left me, but there was no way to escape the beauty of the stranger who stood before me. He was tanned and shining, face strong and gentle, body tall, hard, powerful.

"Got a room?" he said, rolling a toothpick around in his mouth.

"Pardon?" I asked. My mother's zeal for food and cleanliness stretched itself to include language. She never let anyone forget that she had once been a schoolteacher.

"Got a room? I bin lookin' all over. I'm workin' on th' new road, and need a boardin' place."

I hardly heard what he said, I was that busy looking. Even the toothpick wove a spell for me, probably because of the way his lips moved around it.

"Well?" He grinned. "Cat got yer tongue?"

"Just a minute," I said, and went to deliver his message to my mother.

"Certainly not!" she snapped, wiping the flour off her hands with a damp cloth. "As if I didn't have enough to do as it is."

I wanted to get down on my knees and plead. Please, Mother. I'll do anything, if you'll just keep him. I'll come home from school and cook his meals. I'll do his laundry. Only please, Mom. Can't we let him stay, for a little while anyway, just so I can *look* at him?

She came to the door, still wiping her hands. The toothpick was missing, and the beautiful stranger stood before her, quiet, still. I watched her, hope waning. But a flicker remained. I knew that we needed money. I also knew that my brother's room was empty. I stayed close to her, as though hoping that some of my eagerness would seep into her.

Even in her apron, with the white kerchief tied around her hair, my mother was a pretty woman. At forty, she still had a young face and firm skin. She was tanned from hours of blueberry picking and from weeding the garden, and the only flaw in her face was a line between her brows—a mark of worry or of irritation that came and went. She reached the door, the line intact. And then her face changed. I cannot say how it changed. The line was still there, and she was not smiling. But for a few moments, there was something about her that was unfamiliar to me.

Then she said, with more courtesy than I would have expected, "I'm sorry, but I have four children at home, and too much work to do already. You could try Mrs. Schultz across the way."

"I tried Mrs. Schultz," he said. "I tried everyone. I bin everywhere. I even bin to Mr. Snow and asked him if I could sleep in th' barn. Please, ma'am,"—he smiled—"I wouldn't be no bother. I could cook my own meals. Just a room would be fine."

"Well . . ." she said slowly, as though to herself, "there's Jeffrey's room empty, now that he's away in Upper Canada . . ." Then she was silent for a moment or two, staring across the bay, with that line deep between her eyebrows.

"Yes," she said suddenly, but sighing. "I guess we could manage. But you'll eat with us." No way she'd be letting any stranger go messing around in her kitchen. "Will you be needing the room for long, Mr. . . . ?" she inquired.

"No, ma'am," he answered. "Two months maybe. Could be three. Nothin' you can do, once the frost hits hard. Manuel. Manuel Jenkins. I'm much obliged."

He picked up his suitcase and walked in, filling the kitchen with his beauty; blessing the walls, casting light and gladness upon stove, table, electric clock. Like one of the wheeling gulls, I flew out into the back field and up, up to the top of the hill, running all the way. There I threw myself down among the high grasses and the late goldenrod, face turned to the sky. Nothing mattered. Nothing. My mother could crab and fuss and complain all she wanted. My dad could roll over like the Jacksons' yellow dog and wait to be kicked, for all I cared. The beautiful stranger had come and would live in my brother's room for two months. I would hear him moving about next door to me, doing his mysterious ablutions. Through the vent I could maybe hear him breathing. He would be there at suppertime, casting a benediction upon us by his presence, with his smile, his dark skin, his enormous hands with their oddly graceful fingers. I turned over and pressed my face into the grass, blinded by so bright a vision.

∾

Our first meal with Manuel Jenkins was an event to remember. My mother sat at one end of the table, straight as a stick, company manners written all over her face. My father sat at the other end, comfortable, relaxed, slumped in his chair, waiting for the mashed turnips to reach him. When they did, he lit into his food as though, if he didn't attack it immediately, it would vanish from the plate. My mother often reprimanded him about this. "I've spent a long hour and a half preparing this meal," she'd say. "There's no law that says it has to disappear in nothing flat." Or "This is a dining room, Harvey Nickerson, not a barn." To which he paid not the slightest heed whatsoever. It seemed to be the one area where she couldn't move him. Tonight I looked at him and thought, C'mon, Dad. Just for the next couple of months, let's eat slowly, like fancy people. Mr. Jenkins is here. What will he think if we eat like savages?

What indeed? I looked across the table at Mr. Jenkins, and watched him stuff his napkin in the neck of his T-shirt, revealing a veritable carpet of black hairs upon his chest. Then he ate. Holding the fork in his fist like a trowel, he shovelled Mom's enormous meal into himself in perhaps five minutes. And noisily, with quite a lot of smacking and chomping. And when drinking his hot tea, slurping. I didn't mind. He could have eaten his entire meal with his bare hands, and it would have been all the same to me. But I dared not look at my mother. She would never allow anyone to live in our house with table manners like that. Then out came the toothpick, and I watched entranced as it wandered around his mouth without the aid of his fingers. It was as though it had a life of its own. Then he wiped his mouth with the back of his hand, pulled one of Polly's pigtails, smiled his dazzling smile, scraped his chair back, and said, "Much obliged, ma'am. That was some good." And was gone.

I looked at my mother. What would she say, feel, do? Mr. Jenkins had just spent the mealtime doing everything we had always been forbidden to do. Would she make him leave? Would she hate him? But she was just sitting there, arms and hands slack, staring at the tablecloth, registering nothing. After all, she had said he could stay. If she kept her word, she was stuck with him. The younger kids, who had spent half an hour with him before dinner, were all aglow, loving his cheerfulness, his handsome face, his bigness, his booming laugh.

Then he was back.

"S'cuse me, ma'am," he said, "I'm forgettin' m' manners. This here's a lot o' people and a lot o' food. Like you said this morning, you're a hard-workin' lady. You must be some tired." Then he picked up his dishes from the table, washed them in the kitchen sink, and placed them with amazing delicacy in the dish drainer to dry. "Why, thank you, Mr. Jenkins," said Mom, her face expressionless, although for a moment the line disappeared from between her eyebrows. But I remembered his dirty fingernails, and I wondered how she felt about having them in her clean dishwater. Later, I saw her change the water before she washed the other dishes.

"Seems like a nice enough man," said my father, as he stuffed his pipe full of tobacco. Then he pushed away the dishes on the table, to make room for a game of crib with Julien.

∾

We were given three and one-half months with Mr. Jenkins. The frost kept off; and the early winter was as mild as April. We had him with us until January 6th. Three months, fifteen days, and six hours.

Except for my father, we all called him Mr. Jenkins. He was, my mother surmised, about thirty-eight years old, and therefore we were to treat him with the respect befitting an older man—although we all called Aggie Crowell's grandmother Susie, and old Sam was always Sam to us kids. I tried to keep my face inscrutable, but maybe Mom saw the glint in my eye and wanted to place distance between me and him. In any case, I used to call him Manuel privately, when I was alone in my room. "Manuel, Manuel," I would whisper, rolling the name around my tongue, loving the sound, the taste of it.

But it didn't really matter what she made us call him. Calling a man mister couldn't change the way the rest of us felt about him. Even my dad. I think even he was half in love with that towering stranger, in a way that had nothing to do with sex. He grew to love him the way you love a rocky cliff or a heron in flight or a sunfish turning its giant body on the surface of the sea. Or a clown dancing on the street in the midday sun.

Most of us, of course, didn't see him too often. All the kids except Polly were in school, and that just left weekends and suppertime and a small slice of evening, before he'd go up to his room to look at his *Popular Mechanics* magazines and listen to his radio. And my dad was always off fishing by six A.M., gone all day. Mr. Jenkins got his lunch at our place, but no one was there except my mother and Polly and the dog, unless it was on weekends.

Weekends were heaven for me. He didn't have much to do with me directly. But I watched as he made our home a sunshiny place, filling our little house with his huge and animal grace, his laughter, his easy way with life and living. He's like an enormous cat, I thought, a panther, maybe. Working when necessary but knowing how to relax, how to play, how to soak up the sun, letting his cubs crawl all over him as he radiates serenity. Our kids all followed him around like the Pied Piper, and he never seemed to mind. Polly was four, and he'd sit with her on his lap and talk to her as though she were twenty-five years of age. "How was your day, Polly girl?" he'd ask, and then he'd really listen when she told him about her dolls and the dog and the

drawings she had made. I wondered about her sitting on
his dirty overalls in her clean dresses, but my mother made
no comment. Politeness to guests was almost as high on
her list as cleanliness.

Julien had Mr. Jenkins up on a pedestal so high that it's
a wonder he didn't fall off. The two of them would go out
before supper and play catch, and once Mr. Jenkins took
him to show him the front-end loader he worked on. He
let Julien sit way up on top in the driver's seat, and waited
around for a whole half hour while Julien pretended he
was driving it. When Julien came home, his eyes were like
pie plates.

Even Sarah. Gabby old Sarah who never shut up. He'd
sit on the old swing with her, chewing a blade of grass,
while she'd talk on and on and on. And he'd smile and
nod, saying things like "That so?" or "Well, *well,*" or "I
bet you enjoyed *that!*" Never once did he fall asleep in the
middle of all that talk, which is what all the rest of us
always wanted to do. And Mr. Jenkins was a man who
could fall asleep on the head of a pin in the middle of a
thunderstorm, if he wanted to.

Happy though I was, I never got over the small niggling
fear that Mom would finally make him leave, because of
all the bad things he did. He left his shoes around where
you could trip over them, although I tried to protect
him—and us—by putting them by the doorway every time
I found them in the wrong place. He chewed gum with his
mouth open, and passed some around for all of us to do
the same. My mother would chew hers with her small

mouth tightly shut, slowly, as though it tasted either very good or very bad—I could never be sure which. And his belongings—his magazines, his clothes, his tools—littered the house, or decorated it, depending on your point of view—from top to bottom and side to side. My mom, I thought, must have needed that board money really badly.

One evening, early on, during maybe the third week of his stay, my father came home extra tired from lobstering. It had been a day of driving rain, and he was chilled to the bone and grey with fatigue. Everyone was supposed to take off shoes and boots at the door, and he always did; but on that day he sort of moved like a person in a trance, right into the middle of the kitchen floor. My mother flew at him and pushed him backwards to the doorway, her voice hard, as if it were hammering on something metal.

"Inconsiderate! Always inconsiderate! Not one thought for the length of time it takes to scrub a floor! You get out into the back porch and take those wet clothes off before the kitchen looks like a slum. And hurry. Dinner's ready. You're late! I'm not going to wait two more seconds." My dad just stood there for a moment as though he had been struck physically, and then he turned toward the porch.

Then Mr. Jenkins spoke.

"Jest a sweet minute, ma'am," he said, his voice soft and coaxing. "We all knows you works hard. We're all right grateful to you for your good food and all that scrubbin' and polishin'. But anyone can see with half an eye that that man o' yours is three-quarters gone with bein' tired." He said all this in a lazy quiet way, but his eyes, always so kind and warm, were steely cold and serious as death.

"Now, Sarah girl," he went on, "you jest get up and wash them few dirty spots off your mom's floor. Won't take but a minute. And Julien—I think your dad could use your help. Maybe you could put his wet boots out behind the stove to dry them out a bit. And you, m'girl," he said, turning to me, "how about a bottle o' beer for your dad, before he falls right over dead." He said all this from the couch by the back window. He never moved a muscle. Just sort of organized the whole lot of us into a rescue brigade. I thought that would be the end of Mr. Jenkins. I'd never my whole life long heard anyone tell my mother to shut up, and that's really what he was doing. But she just turned quickly back to the stove and started shoving pots around, this way and that. When we all finally sat down to supper, there wasn't any tension left at all—not in me, anyway. Mr. Jenkins sat up, talking with his mouth full, and told us about life up in the James Bay territory when he was working on the new highway up there. His huge brown body, sandwiched between Julien and Polly, was like one of the statues I'd seen in our ancient history book. I was sick with longing for him, but also oddly content just to sit peacefully at a distance and feast my eyes upon his grace of body and person. For me, the slurp of his tea was like background music. I always avoided my mother's eyes at the dinner table. As time went by, I knew she would not evict him, but I felt I could not bear it if she scolded him, like us, for his table manners.

When Christmastime came, Mr. Jenkins said he was leaving for the four-day holiday. The kids all kicked up a terrible row, and my dad begged him to stay. "Surely they can do without you at home just this one year," he said.

"Well," said Mr. Jenkins, grinning sheepishly, "truth to tell, home is where I hangs my hat at any given time. If you wants me to stay, that I will do, thanking you most kindly." Then he excused himself and took the bus to Yarmouth, and was gone for ten hours.

On Christmas Day, we found out what he had done with those ten hours. He had gone shopping. And shopping and shopping. He bought extra lights for the tree and a wreath for the door. He supplied a bottle of real champagne and another of sparkling wine that I was allowed to taste, and there was pink lemonade for the kids. He had even bought tall glasses with stems—seven of them—for all of us. He gave Polly a doll that said six different things when you pulled a string in her back. For Julien he had an exact model of his front-end loader, and I thought Julien might possibly faint for joy. Sarah got three Nancy Drew books, and for me he bought a silver bracelet with "Sterling" written inside it. He gave my dad a big red wool sweater to keep him warm in the lobster boat, no matter how cold it got. To my mother, he presented a gold chain with a small amethyst pendant. We all had gifts for him, too, either bought or made or cooked, and the day was one of the single most perfect days I have ever known.

If Christmas was a perfect day, the day that came two weeks later was a terrible one. We all knew he had to leave soon, that the deep frost wouldn't stay away forever. But when he actually stood there in the kitchen, holding his suitcase, it seemed that all that was warm and beautiful in our lives was about to abandon us. I could not imagine the supper table without him, the couch empty, the silence that would strike me from Jeffrey's room. He shook hands with my dad and my mother. My dad pumped his hand and said, "Come again, Manuel, and good luck." My mother stood erect as ever, and said, "It was a pleasure to have you here, Mr. Jenkins," and almost sounded as though she meant it. Polly and Sarah cried, and he hugged them both. Then he tossed Julien up in the air and shook his hand. Julien didn't say a single word, because it took his whole strength just to keep from crying. Then Mr. Jenkins came and shook my hand and kissed me lightly on the top of my head. "Have a good life, m'girl," he said, and smiled such a smile at me, oh such a smile. Then he walked to the door.

A lot is said about the value of strong, silent men. Me, I think that men who are silent about things that matter just don't have the strength to say what they really feel. Manuel Jenkins turned around at the doorway and said, "Thank you. I'll be missing you a whole lot. I loves you all." Then he was gone. I put on my warm jacket and boots and went back to the old sawmill and sat inside on a bench. Over by the breakwater, the gulls were screaming, screaming, and I could hear the winter wind rattling the broken windows. I had taken several of my dad's big handkerchiefs with me, because I knew I was going to be doing a lot of crying.

The whole family just sort of limped through the next few weeks, but gradually we emerged from our grief and got on with our lives. My mother would say things like "My word, he was only a man. Perk up, Julien. It isn't the end of the world." Or to Polly and Sarah, "For goodness' sake, stop sighing. At least we're not falling all over his shoes, and there's a lot less work for me to do." And to my dad, "Don't look so sad, Harvey. He's not the only one on earth who can play crib. C'mon. I'll have a game with you." One day she said to me, not unkindly, right out of the blue, "He was too old for you. You'll find your own man sometime, and he'll be right for you. Let Mr. Jenkins go." I wasn't even mad. I didn't know why.

One day in late February I was sent home from school with a high fever. The vice-principal drove me to the front gate. I entered the house by the back door and took off my boots in the porch. Then, slowly, because I was not feeling well, I dragged myself upstairs. At the top of the stairs I stopped short, unable to go forward or back. There, to the right of me, beyond her doorway, was my mother, sitting in front of her dressing table. Her forehead was right down on the table top and was lying on her left hand. The other hand was stretched out across the top, and was in a tight fist. I was very frightened. I had never before seen my mother in any state of weakness whatsoever. She seemed never to be sick, nor had I ever heard her give voice to any physical pain. She was always strong, sure, in perfect control. A heart attack, I thought, and dared not speak lest I alarm her. Then, as I waited, a long terrible sigh shook her, and she opened her closed fist. Then she closed it and sighed again. In her hand was the gold chain and the amethyst pendant.

I crept down the stairs in my stocking feet and put on my outdoor clothes in the back porch. Then I retraced my steps to the front gate, fever and all, and slammed it shut. Returning to the back porch, I stomped the snow off my feet on the stoop and entered the house, banging the door behind me. I was long and slow taking my clothes off, and by the time I was hanging up my scarf, my mother appeared in the kitchen.

"What's wrong?" she said, her voice warm and concerned. "Why are you home so early?" I realized for the first time that she had become gentler, and that she had been like that for a long time. Even to my father. Possibly especially to my father. As I mounted the stairs to bed, I pondered these things, but none of them made much sense to me.

You maybe thought I was telling you this tale about Mr. Manuel Jenkins because there was something secret and terrible in his past that we eventually found out about. But no. Or possibly you were looking for something dramatic at the end, like the Mounties coming to get him, or a tragic death under the front-end loader. But none of those things happened. He just came. And then he just went. None of us, not one of us, ever saw him again. He never wrote to us, which seemed odd to me at the time, because he was a great one for saying thank you. So I think now that perhaps he didn't know how to write.

Maybe those big hands of his never held a pencil. Come to think of it, he never would join the kids when they did their crossword puzzles. "Too hard for me," he'd say, chuckling, and we always thought he was joking. No. He just left. Disappeared down the road in his front-end loader, and was swallowed up by the hill behind Mrs. Fitzgerald's house.

I'm forty-one years old now, and from time to time I still ache to see Manuel Jenkins. I'm happily married to a husband whom I love most dearly, and I have four beautiful children. But I feel as though something is unfinished. Does that seem curious to you? It's like seeing a really great movie and having to leave the theatre ten minutes before the end. Or like wanting a teddy bear all your whole life long and not ever having one. Or like yearning to see, one more time, the rocky coast where you grew up. And I'm exactly the age my mother was when he left. Sometimes I think that if I could see him just once more, I might understand everything, all of it. And that then I could put the memory of him away where it belongs. Although I live on a farm in the middle of Saskatchewan, I have a notion that one of these days I'll just turn around, and there he'll be at the back door, filling the kitchen with his size and with his grace.

It could happen, you know. I feel it could.

My War

"I love the war." My lips formed the words, but there was no sound. Although young, I knew that it was an indecent thing to love the war. I was not entirely stupid. I knew that fathers and brothers died, and occasionally sisters. Newspapers and the radio brought news every day of ships sinking, cities being bombed, widows weeping, children bereft. It was unthinkable to love the war, and there I was doing it. So I felt guilty; I told no one, but I allowed myself the luxury of my own private feelings. The time was 1941, during some of the darkest days of the Second World War. The place was Halifax, in Nova Scotia. I was fourteen years old.

Later, I was to realize that the First and Second World Wars were not, after all, so very far apart. My own father had returned from the first one, just twenty-one years before the second one began. I know now that twenty-one years is a very short time. When I was fourteen, it seemed like an endless stretch of years. It was history. It was the past. And the past was not attractive to me unless it could be made to seem vivid, dramatic. Thus, it mystified and infuriated me that my father refused to talk about his own war. Why? I wanted to hear colourful tales of brave deeds on the battlefields, long heroic marches over treacherous terrain, the mournful sounds of the last post, stoicism in the face of extreme pain.

"Tell me about it," I'd beg. "Describe to me what it was like. *Please,* Dad."

But he would tell me nothing. His face would take on what I came to call his "war mask," and he'd say, "Sorry, Lisa. I'm just not ready to talk about it."

Ready! If he wasn't ready after twenty-one years, what were the possibilities of his *ever* being ready? When I watched him listening to the news on the day that war was declared in 1939, I think I knew that day would never come. When he rose from his chair to leave the room (the warm September sun streaming through the window, lighting up the pots of blazing geraniums on the sill)—his face bleak, his shoulders slumped—I could see that he was crying.

What a surprise, then, to find so much to enjoy in this new war. The streets of Halifax—damp and grey for so long—were suddenly alive with laughing sailors, jaunty in their bell-bottom trousers and cocky hats. With my best friend, Daisy, I cruised through the busy sidewalks of the downtown, agape at this spectacle. We listened to the energetic voices of the Wrens, who swung along Barrington Street in their snappy outfits, conscious of new roles for themselves, new power; our eager adolescent eyes feasted on the handsome men lounging on the stone walls of the Grand Parade, sporting uniforms from countries I'd scarcely heard of. The waters of Bedford Basin were constantly crammed with scores of ships, awaiting departure for mysterious and dangerous places. And the silent, secret convoys, slipping out of the Basin and along the harbour, never failed to move me. Daisy and I pored over pictures of ships struggling through heavy waves on winter seas, superstructures layered with ice, men clinging to the handrails, their faces grim.

∽

How I longed to be on one of those ships, bound for adventures that I was sure I could easily cope with. I pictured myself limping bravely through foreign streets, strewn with the debris left behind by bombs: broken glass; piles of brick and powdered plaster; barefaced buildings open like dolls' houses, whole walls torn away; people bent over, searching through the rubble for lost belongings. But I was fine. In spite of my limp (some sort of wound was always featured in these scenes), ignoring my gnawing hunger, I was marching ahead with purpose and strength. A nurse? (Carrying my black bag, on my way to the overcrowded hospital, its corridors loud with cries of torment.) A spy? (Lurking in dark alleyways, clutching my case of coded documents, sliding along with my back to the wall, alert, *ready*.) A member of the Canadian Women's Army Corps? (Erect, neglecting my injuries, my uniform torn and marked by splinters and dirt—and blood?—nonetheless complementing my excellent figure.) I didn't have an excellent figure in 1941, but inaccuracies never impeded the forward movement of my dreams, by day or by night. And no suffering presented itself that I was unable to bear, no task was too difficult or too dangerous.

Real life in Halifax could be almost as dramatic as my fantasies. I revelled in the murky nights, made dark by thousands of sets of blackout curtains. I was thrilled by the searchlights practising in the sky, chasing the tiny silver planes, catching them, losing them, sweeping across the night sky with their giant fingers. I took pleasure in the crowded streets, the reeling drunks, laughing, singing; in the sight of the drab old city, dressed up, brought alive— yet again—by a global conflict. Yes, I loved the war.

In other ways, life continued on much as before. Basically, I guess I was fond of my family, but they all irritated me with varying degrees of intensity. My father, shell-shocked in the First World War, had a remoteness about him that was difficult to penetrate, and I resented this. My mother was sensitive and loving, but far too concerned about my safety and happiness. My brother, Jeremy, was a full-fledged ten-year-old pest—showing off, teasing me, tormenting the cat, eating more than his share of everything. But then there was Daisy.

Daisy called for me each weekday morning, and we walked to school, talking and talking—discussing the teachers' various peculiarities, picking flaws in our friends, condemning the intricacies of mathematics. In late afternoon, we did our homework together at alternate houses. Afterwards, on the telephone, we described the servicemen and women who had come to our houses for last Sunday's dinner. We complained about the absurd restrictions set up by our parents. (My mother, for example, forbade me to walk in Point Pleasant Park, the 186 acres of woods in the south of Halifax, or in Marlboro Woods, unless accompanied by an adult—all this, in spite of my impatient assurances to her that I was exceptionally strong and could easily fend off any attacker.) We discussed, with admiration, jealousy, and scorn, the peculiarities of the English Guest Children who attended our school, safe from the bombs, but not from the hazards of Canadian peer pressure and incompatible foster homes.

Daisy and I also talked about boys, sex, and the future possibilities of love. In spite of the surrounding hordes of handsome servicemen, both of us were deeply in love with Mr. Grant, our new history teacher. He was rumoured to be exceptionally fond of his dark-haired wife, and he also had a small daughter of whom he was said to be extravagantly proud. None of this prevented us from creating elaborate daydreams centred around his secret attraction to me or to Daisy. In spite of a severe football injury which had kept him out of the war, he was built like an Olympic athlete—tall, strong, young. He was a teacher, but also a listener (rare, we felt, among teachers), with a head of dishevelled and agonizingly appealing blond hair. Daisy and I ached, we longed, we lusted for Mr. Grant.

Once or twice he brought his little daughter to school with him, because of some crisis at home—illness, the death of an in-law, failure to obtain a sitter. Her name was Abigail, and she was three years old. She would sit up at a little table which he'd brought along with him, cutting out shapes (badly), drawing scribbly, undecipherable pictures, leafing through a pile of picture books, sometimes talking out loud, but quietly, to herself.

From time to time, Abigail would stop to listen, or just to look—watching her father as he wrote assignments on the blackboard or described to us the social customs of the early Romans. She also scrutinized the students—solemnly, her eyes level and interested, taking it all in. She had blond hair like her father's, curly like her mother's. Her large blue eyes were framed by a fringe of dark lashes. She was very beautiful, and I admitted to myself that if Mr. Grant were to reject his wife and opt for me, I would be happy to accept Abigail as part of the bargain. In any case, it was clear that this would be necessary. Even while discussing the marriage rituals and dietary habits of the Romans, his eyes kept focusing on that little table, gazing at Abigail with a love that was public and poignant. I hoped he would look at my own children—*our* own children—in the same way.

One day, very late on a December afternoon, Daisy and I meandered home after basketball practice. We talked, laughed, complained about our parents, chewed gum loudly and with our mouths open, pulling long strings of it out at arm's length and then tossing back our heads to reel it back in.

"Dis*gus*ting!" I said, through three separate wads of gum.

"But delightful," said Daisy, as the last grey strool of gum was sucked back in.

It was delicious to be out in the early evening now that the days had become so short. The heavy darkness of the blackout pressed in on us, but the rising full moon was beginning to pick up details in our surroundings. The edges of the Morrisons' silver birch were, indeed, silver. A ghostly blue light shone on the white wooden houses, the bare branches, people's faces.

A practice air-raid siren—which we'd learned to ignore—almost drowned out the scream of a fire engine. But we heard it. A fire! Daisy and I were avid fire-watchers, and never missed a major fire unless extraordinary circumstances prevented us from attending—as when the Queen Hotel burned down during the week I had chicken pox. But we could certainly enjoy this one. It was nearby. We could tell. The sirens had whined to a stop, and we could see a pink glow reflected on the Jacobsons' roof. A familiar eagerness squeezed my chest.

We didn't have to speak. In unison, we raced in the direction of the sounds of shouts, unreeling hoses, clattering ladders. And came to a stop, facing a four-storey boxlike apartment building on a South End street. The firemen were already affixing hoses to the hydrant, racing in and out of the front door, shouting instructions and information to one another. The deepening red reflection on the Jacobsons' house was coming from the apartment building's third floor. Flames were visible behind three of the windows and belched out of a fourth. Bedraggled tenants were stumbling out of the side and front entrances, men staggering under the weight of valuables (I could see a painting of the Peggy's Cove lighthouse, a briefcase, a flat box for storing silverware, a stack of photo albums, a ragged-looking teddy bear), women carrying babies, children crying. On the fourth floor, windows were being shoved open, and smoke was starting to curl slowly through the openings and underneath the roof.

I grabbed Daisy's wrist. "Daisy!" I yelled above the din. "Mr. Grant lives in there!"

Daisy's fist flew to her mouth, and she shouted into my ear. "Yes! And on the fourth floor!" She'd gone there once to deliver an essay. We both stood unmoving, scarcely breathing, scanning the exits for the three familiar faces, watching the windows through the gathering smoke. Ladders were already being moved into place, to rescue a family that had appeared at a corner window. One by one they came down, agonizingly slowly.

Suddenly I clutched Daisy's arm again. "Look!" I whispered, and pointed to the middle window. There they were: Mr. Grant, his face frantic; his wife, her eyes wild; their screaming daughter. The ladders were in use elsewhere. There was nothing there for them. Between coughing fits, they called for help and struggled to keep Abigail from racing back into the room. Then we could see the three of them leaning out beyond the windowsill, obviously trying to find some air they could hope to breathe, Mr. Grant holding Abigail as far out of the smoke as possible.

All of a sudden, one of the ladders slammed against the wall beside their window, jarring one of his arms loose from Abigail. For a long moment, he struggled to hold her with his free arm, unable to reach her with his other. Then, as if in slow motion (or so it seemed to me later), she slipped out of his grasp and started her awful journey to the pavement, far below. When she landed, she was as close to me as if she had been on the other side of my own living room. I heard the appalling sound as she struck the sidewalk. I watched it. I saw all of it, all the horror of what there was to see. When I tore my eyes away long enough to look at the window again, Mr. Grant was gone. Where? He would never be able to get through that inferno of the third floor to reach ground level. But he did. He raced out the front door, fire licking at his trousers, his sleeves. Firemen had to stop him forcibly, in order to turn the hose on him to put out the flames.

Then he walked over to what was left of his daughter, slowly now, like a sleepwalker. He knelt down, picked up her body, and held it in his arms. Then he raised his head up to the sky and made sounds that I had never before heard coming from a human being—long wails of anguish, like a large animal in mortal pain. I stared up at the window again. Mrs. Grant was being carried down the ladder by a fireman, draped like a sack of flour over his shoulder, her eyes closed.

By the time I looked again at Mr. Grant, someone had placed Abigail's body on a stretcher and covered it with a sheet. Mr. Grant was kneeling on the pavement, curled over with his head against his knees, pulling at his hair. The animal sounds continued, but lower, slower. Off to the side, I could see an ambulance attendant approaching him. Or a doctor, maybe.

By now, the entire building was ablaze. "C'mon," I croaked to Daisy. "I'm leaving."

On the way home, Daisy was full of talk. Agonized talk, shocked talk, but nonetheless talk. I thought I might kill her if she said one more word.

"Shut up, Daisy!" I shouted. "Just shut up!" Then I broke away and ran back to the school, stumbling over curbs on the street, and over bits and pieces of play equipment in the school yard. Finally, I found the little kids' jungle gym and sat down underneath it, curled up in the fetal position, holding my chest with both of my arms. I rocked back and forth, moaning rather than crying, my mind a confusion of images and fear. I kept muttering over and over again, "Please, God. Please, God. Please, God." Please *what?* I had no idea.

After a time, with a kind of consuming fatigue that was new to me, I rose from my cramped position and stood up. The moon was well above the horizon now, and it was no longer difficult to see. Slowly I walked home, staring at the sidewalk, trying not to think, talking to myself. What I said was: "Empty. Empty. Empty."

When I opened up the front door of my house, there was visible relief on everyone's face, even on Jeremy's. Where had I been? Why hadn't I called? Didn't I realize how worried they'd be?

I realized no such thing. I cared nothing for their worry. I didn't answer them. I walked straight upstairs and lay face downward on my bed. I could hear my father outside my door, saying to my mother. "She saw it all. Daisy said so. No one should see anything like that at the age of fourteen. I think we should leave her alone for a while."

⁓

Mercifully, the next day was Saturday. It was therefore not yet necessary to face school and all the eager questions people would ask—with shock, with sorrow, with relish. Jeremy shut himself up in the den with his Meccano set. Obviously, he'd been warned to keep out of my way.

I looked with uncustomary fondness at my father, who was sitting in his favourite armchair, reading *The Halifax Chronicle*.

"I'm sorry, Dad," I said. It was the first time I had spoken since returning home the previous night.

He looked up, puzzled. "Sorry about what?"

"I'm not sure," I said. "About your war and all. Yes. About your war."

His brows were squeezed together, but he smiled at me.

My mother approached me with cornflakes, which I pushed aside. Not angrily. It was just that I knew I couldn't eat them.

"I know it was very bad," she said.

"Yes," I said. "It was bad."

Then I spoke again. "Mrs. Grant. Is she alive?"

"Yes," she said. "But in shock."

"Yes," I whispered. "In shock."

"Lisa," my mother said. "From our attic window, I can see a convoy going out. I know how you love to see them. Do you want to go up on Citadel Hill and watch?" I sensed that she could hardly bear to see me like this.

"No," I said. "Sorry, Mom, but I don't think I want the war today." Or maybe any other day, I thought. As I sat there in front of my uneaten cornflakes, I let the war go. I released it with reluctance, but I let it pass out of me and into some other space where it belonged. I was picking balls of fluff off my sweater.

"Sweetheart," my mother urged, voice low, eyes kind. "Would you like to talk about it?"

"Maybe sometime," I said. "Thanks, Mom, but right now I guess I'm not quite ready."

Then I went upstairs and lay on the bed for a long time, staring at the ceiling, thinking. After a while, I got up, crossed over to my desk, sat down, and started to do my history homework.

Brothers and Sisters

On the other side of the sand dunes, the sun shone down on a turbulent sea. Its surface was broken by whitecaps, which raced toward the northern point of land, crashing on the granite rocks in an explosion of white breakers and spray. On the beach, the waves pounded onto the sand, and then inhaled into themselves, dragging a multitude of rattling pebbles out into the undertow. What's more, both sea and sky were a dazzling blue. It was what most sea-people would describe as a perfect day.

Sylvia MacIsaac was a sea-person. She'd lived close to this beach all her life, and she couldn't imagine living anywhere else. She didn't know how people from inland survived without the sea at their doorsteps to soothe or invigorate them.

But today Sylvia felt neither soothed nor invigorated.

She didn't even turn her head to check out the surf on the Western Ledges—reefs that were throwing up water like giant geysers. No. Her eyes were on the ground as she kicked her way through the tough dune grasses that grew in the sand behind the beach. She stomped along, dry-eyed but grieving, teeth clenched hard together. Sylvia was too preoccupied to notice the beauty of the day. She was busy hating her sister.

Finally Sylvia found her favourite spot, which she'd called her "secret hideout" ever since she'd been a little girl. It was a patch of sand about six feet in diameter, surrounded by a waving tangle of tall beach grasses. For some reason, the spot had never filled in with any of the dry vegetation that grew on the dunes. There it was, an almost perfect circle of sand, year after year. Sylvia had long ago stopped playing pirate or mermaid on that section of sand, but even at the age of sixteen, she often came here—to sulk, to fume, to think, to exult, or just to be alone with herself. Sylvia *needed* that patch of empty dune. She even came here in winter, lying down on the sand or snow in her warm jacket and pants, her earmuffs on and her fingers curled up inside her mittens. Closing her eyes, she would let the sound of the thundering surf occupy her head.

Today it was mid-July, but it was cold on the beach. However, when she reached her special spot, she plopped down on the sand, knowing she'd be warm, confident that the long stretches of beach grasses would keep the wind away. She placed the palm of her hand on the sand. Yes, it was very warm, almost hot. In spite of her fury, Sylvia smiled.

But she didn't smile for long. She was busy dredging up the past and cursing the present. She could hear the power of the breaking waves from her small protected spot, muffled and deep. The sound was a perfect accompaniment to her mood.

She'd seen him first. It wasn't fair. She'd watched him get out of the car, loaded down with boxes, and walk into the old Grimsby house—followed by a pair of tall parents, a kid sister, and a weird-looking gangly brother who wore glasses as thick as telescopes. Stationed behind the slits in the bathroom blinds, Sylvia had watched all of this through a pair of binoculars.

He was everything she'd ever dreamed about, and she did a lot of fantasizing—on the dunes, in bed, or in school when chemistry was boring her. He was quite tall, with a shock of thick black hair, a big smile (even while carrying boxes) and perfect features. His family was moving into that empty house, and it was *next door*. She'd heard that they were from British Columbia. That was exotic enough. But she hadn't expected or even hoped for a third-millennium Greek god. And because she was the very first person to see him, she intended to reserve him for her very own.

The next day, the moving van arrived. Sylvia wondered what they'd slept on the night before. Her mother had taken over a hamburger casserole and a plate of brownies, but you can't sleep on those. Sleeping bags, probably. Her mother had come back all smiles.

"A really pleasant family," she said. "Joseph and Maria Manzano, and three nice kids."

Nice, Sylvia thought. Find me a better word to describe perfection.

"The little girl is called Adriana. Her brothers are Carlos and Marcus. The boys'll be going to your high school."

"Which is which?" Sylvia whispered.

"Carlos is the good-looking one," she said. "The long drink of water with glasses is Marcus."

Carlos. Carlos. Sylvia said the name over and over again in her mind. *Such a name.*

"From Mexico, one generation back," said her mother. "And then B.C. They moved here from the West Coast to escape all that rain. I guess Mexicans need a lot of sun. But Maria said they also needed to live beside the sea."

"It rains here, too," Sylvia said. "Remember last April?" They might move if it got to be too wet. Already she was nervous about that possibility.

"I remember," said Mom. "But no way was I going to tell them that on the very first day they moved in."

"What's he do?" said Dad, from behind *The Chronicle Herald.*

"Computer experts, both of them," said Mom. "Found the old Grimsby house on the Internet. Their jobs are in Dartmouth. Maybe we can carpool in with them. You could take the ferry to the other side."

Sylvia went upstairs to lie on her bed so that she could think about Carlos without any interruptions. Her daydreams came thick and fast. *Carlos and me sunbathing on the beach. I'm short, but my waist is minuscule and I have good boobs. Showing him the Halifax Citadel, holding his hand to keep from falling into the moat. Watching the Buskers Festival with him. Sitting with him on the stone wall by the Halifax Library, eating french fries and listening to the guitar player. Going swimming by moonlight.* Sylvia got up off the bed and looked at herself in the full-length mirror. Not great, she thought, but not at all bad, either. An okay face, long, straight brown hair, brown eyes, tanned skin, big smile. She smiled at herself in the mirror. *We'd make an attractive couple. And no doubt Mexicans have an eye for people who are dark skinned.*

Judith was standing in the doorway of her room. "Who are you smiling at?" she asked. "Pleased with what you see?"

For one blissful hour Sylvia had forgotten about Judith. But there she was, so long and lovely and slender that she looked like some kind of wood nymph, or one of the fairies in *A Midsummer Night's Dream.* With clouds of light blond hair—which curled. Enormous blue eyes. White and perfect skin. Graceful as a deer. To see her was to sink into despair, especially if she was your sister. Sylvia thought about Carlos, and felt a constriction in her chest. *I saw him first. And you don't look too wonderful with a sunburn, Judith. I tan.*

"Have you seen the hunk, next door?" Judith asked, draping herself beguilingly across Sylvia's bed.

"Yes," said Sylvia. She was not beguiled for even a second. She didn't want to discuss any of this.

"I have plans," said Judith as she unwound herself from the bed. Sylvia closed her eyes.

Ten minutes later, they were all in the kitchen preparing the meal. Dad was slicing onions and crying. Mom was spinning the lettuce. Judith was cutting up a Sobey's apple pie and putting the pieces on four plates. Sylvia was setting the table in the dining alcove, muttering *Carlos, Carlos* under her breath, as she put the plates, napkins, glasses and cutlery at each place. Suddenly she heard a voice. It was Judith's. "Hey, Mom," she was saying. "All those rolls—that's more than we need for supper. How be I take a few over to the starving Manzanos?"

"Well," said Mom, "they're not exactly starving. I fed them their supper yesterday, and I imagine that two computer experts could afford a restaurant. It only takes ten minutes to get to the Seadog Café." Mom had had a hard day. She taught junior high, and sometimes those kids could be like a pack of wolves.

Then she said, "Forget I said that. I sound like a shrew. Sure. Take them over ten rolls. Two each. I made two dozen. They're still warm. Do it now."

Sylvia watched out the kitchen window as Judith ran across the narrow field to the Manzano house. When the door opened, she disappeared inside. It seemed to Sylvia that she was gone for a very long time. It shouldn't take twenty minutes to deliver ten rolls.

It turned out that what Mexicans truly loved were people with chalk-white skin, curly blond hair and blue eyes. Sylvia was out. Judith was in. Even Mr. and Mrs. Manzano fell in love with her looks, her fabulous grace, her vitality. Within a week, Carlos and Judith were inseparable. They could be seen walking up and down the mill road, arm in arm, hand in hand, her soft paleness and his beautiful darkness complementing each other. Or they would meet at the MacIsaacs' house or the Manzanos' to watch TV, play cribbage, talk. Sylvia felt like a stranger in her own home. She knew she was the ugliest duckling in the pond. But she smiled and smiled, pretending that all was well. Not that Carlos noticed. He couldn't take his eyes off Judith for a split second. From time to time he would reach out and touch Judith's curls, almost reverently, whispering, "I love your hair." When that happened, Sylvia could feel tears stinging the corners of her eyes. One day she looked down at her clenched fists. The knuckles were white.

It was on Saturday that Judith announced (at lunchtime, with her mouth full, as a matter of fact) that Carlos would be in grade twelve in the fall. Sylvia knew she'd hit rock bottom. Judith would be in the same classroom. Sylvia would be going into grade eleven. She shoved her plate away and stalked out of the kitchen, picking up the old plaid beach blanket on her way out of the back porch. She knew where she had to go. To her special place on the dunes. To lick her wounds. She knew deep down that Judith hadn't done anything all that wrong. She'd just been a little too quick on the draw. But Sylvia wanted to slaughter her for being so blond and so beautiful, and for being so consciously, so smugly, charming. And for grabbing those rolls so fast, to use as bait.

∾

Down on the beach, Sylvia had headed for her secret hideout, without looking to right or to left. She was a horse with blinkers on. Never mind that it was the most beautiful day of the entire month of July. She only had eyes for one thing, and it had broad shoulders, velvety dark skin, and an electric smile. Sylvia dumped herself and the blanket down on the sand, and lay, face upwards, staring at the sky. She narrowed her eyes against its blueness, then finally closed them, resigning herself to misery.

Suddenly she could hear the *swish swish* of beach grasses, and she wondered who or what was out there, moving around. A giant gull, a dog, or maybe a beach prowler like herself. *Don't let anyone find my special place.* She kept her eyes closed, as though to do so would prevent any kind of discovery.

The swishing came closer and closer, until all of a sudden she could sense rather than hear a kind of commotion, as someone broke through the grasses on the edge of her small island of sand. Then, *whoever it was* tripped on the edge of her blanket, and fell full-length across her body. Terrified, she lay like a stone, fingers dug into the sand, eyes now widely open, while the intruder gathered together his arms and legs and struggled to rise. All the

while, he was muttering, "Oh my God, my gosh, my God,
I'm sorry! *I'm sorry!*" When he was finally upright, she
dared to look at him. From her position on the ground, he
looked like a giant standing there against the sky, with his
hands covering his eyes, his face. He was still muttering
apologies behind his long fingers, but she remained shocked
and frightened. Grabbing her blanket, she wrapped herself
in it as though to protect herself, now sitting up, knees
close to her chest in a fetal position. He was very close to
her, standing on the same six-foot circle of sand.

Then he took his hands away from his eyes and looked
at her, eyes narrowed. With an agonized cry of "Oh, *no!*
Not *you!*" he sank to his knees and put his hands over his
face again. Sylvia wondered if she should be somehow
extricating herself from her blanket and from all this
madness, and fleeing across the beach to safety. But it was
as though an unseen giant hand were pressing her onto
the sand. Besides, curiosity and fascination were starting
to replace her fear; surely one needn't be afraid of anyone
so apologetic—and with such a wonderful bass voice. By
now, he'd dropped his hands from his face and was
looking at her, sitting back on his heels. "Did I hurt you?"
he said. "Did I break your ribs or smash your pelvis or
anything?"

"I'm okay," she said, taking in the chiseled lines of his
face, the strong cheekbones, his warm brown eyes.

"Where are my glasses?" he muttered, and started
patting the ground like a blind person. It was she who
found them, emerging from her blanket in order to help in

the search. *Glasses!* Could it be? Yes, it could. The brother. Marcus. Marcus of the telescope eyes—now beady and small behind the lenses—stared at her. Then, suddenly, he lifted his face to the sky and started to shake. At first, all that moved were his shoulders, which trembled and heaved uncontrollably. Was he having some kind of fit? Sylvia pulled the blanket close around her again. Then he threw back his head and laughed and laughed until he bent double, holding his stomach. When he was finally able to stop, he muttered to himself—and maybe to her—"The irony! Oh, the irony of it all!"

Sylvia wasn't frightened any longer. This Marcus person might be a little bit crazy, but he certainly wasn't dangerous. After all, he lived in the old Grimsby house, and there was no way he was going to start out his new life in Nova Scotia by assaulting his next-door neighbour. Not on purpose, anyway. She smiled.

"You're *smiling!*" He almost yelled the words. "Why are you *smiling?* What does it mean?"

She laughed. "It means that I just figured out that you're probably not going to rape me!"

He blushed. His skin turned a dark anguished red from the top of his forehead to the neck of his white sweatshirt. She had never before seen a boy or a man blush, and she couldn't have been more surprised (or strangely delighted) if he'd burst into tears. It swept across her mind that probably Carlos had never blushed in his life. Someone that perfect probably had nothing to blush about. Had she ever seen Judith blush? No, she hadn't.

"A perfect pair," she said, not realizing that she'd spoken.

"A perfect what?" Marcus frowned.

She might as well explain. "Judith and Carlos," she said. "My sister and your brother. Beautiful, handsome, confident—a perfect pair."

"Yes," he said, his wonderful voice unmistakably gloomy. "Perfect."

"You were hoping she'd want you, not him." This seemed to be her day for speaking before she'd made any decision about what to say. She felt so depressed that she didn't even care about things like that.

He looked at her and grinned. What a spectacular smile, with all those flashing white Manzano teeth. "Me and Judith? You have to be kidding." Then he threw back his head and laughed again.

"No? Not you and Judith? What's so funny?"

"I watched you both from the window—even before Judith danced in with the rolls, flashing those hot looks at Carlos. When I saw the two of you moving around out there, I thought I'd never seen anyone so graceful."

"Yeah," said Sylvia. "That's what everyone says about her." Why was she feeling so tired?

"Not her. *You.*"

"*What?*"

"Yes. Oh, she's graceful, all right. But she's working too hard at it. You can tell how pleased she is with her charms. Me, I like something a little more subtle. Besides, I've never been attracted to that kind of frizzly blondness." He smiled again, and for a moment she almost forgot about his telescope eyes.

He went on. "I wouldn't be saying all this stuff," he said, "but when you almost kill someone, it sort of loosens your vocal cords."

She laughed. "It's good," she said. "I like it. Guys almost never talk. They're too busy being strong and silent."

"Well," he said, "I'll have to admit I've tried going that route. But it's pretty boring. Besides, there's always too many things I want to talk about."

"Like what?"

"Like that I was scared to death Carlos would go after you. I knew if that happened, I'd never ever have a chance."

You're right, Marcus. You wouldn't have had a hope.

"But then I couldn't figure out how to get through to you. I could tell you hadn't even *seen* me. You had that look on your face that always happens when girls see Carlos for the first time."

"What look?"

"Oh, you know. Sort of stunned. Stupefied by Carlos. You didn't frown at me or anything. You just dismissed me. I know that look, too."

"So?"

"So I came down to the beach to plan the rest of my life." He laughed. "And to try to get rid of my almost perpetual sinking feeling." He stretched his impossibly long legs and arms and said, "Let's walk."

When she stood up beside him, she was amazed by his height. He had to be a foot taller than she was. "Ever play basketball?" she asked.

"No. Blind as a bat. Also, clumsy. I'm so tall that I could reach up and almost *put* the ball in the basket. But I'd have to run around and dribble and pass. Worse still— *catch*. I'd fall flat on my face before I was halfway down the court. Carlos is the athletic one." He frowned. "Of course," he added.

"Doesn't Carlos have *any* flaws?"

"Not many," said Marcus, slowly. "He's even sort of nice—most of the time. A bit conceited, but why not? I'd be incurably conceited if I was him. I'd prance around like one of those show horses." He laughed.

"No flaws at all?"

"Well, let me think. He hates cats. He doesn't like beaches. They probably blow his perfect hair around too much." He frowned again. "Sorry. Scratch that remark from the evidence." He was silent for a while and looked out at the reefs.

Then he continued. "Flaws, you ask. Well, he's got almost zero sense of humour. I couldn't survive for one day if I didn't find a whole lot of stuff funny."

Sylvia looked up at him. "Why did you *really* come to the beach, today?"

"Because I love the beach. Because I was feeling so low, and the sea always makes me feel so high. But mainly because I wanted to plan strategy."

"Strategy?"

"Yeah. How to meet you. What to say to you. How to get you to notice that Carlos has a real nice brother. How to make a good impression. I thought I might start by telling you that I'm getting contact lenses next week."

"Are you?"

"No, but I thought it might be worthwhile to try lying."

It was her turn to laugh. The breakers crashed down on the sand, and she and Marcus took off their sneakers and played tag with the waves. Then they played tag with each other, which was even more fun. He nearly always caught her, of course, but the catching was wonderful. Or she'd dodge around boulders and in and out of the water, and he'd trip and go sprawling onto the sand. Then they'd laugh some more.

After a while they headed for home, hand in hand. The wind caught Sylvia's long slippery hair, tossing it across her face, around her neck. "So much for strategy," she said.

"Yeah," he said. "Next time I want to meet a girl and make a lasting impression, I'll know exactly what to do." Then he reached down, and very gently unwound her hair from around her neck.

"I love your hair," he said.

Brothers, she thought.

Carlotta's Search

Most people would have said that Carlotta Kirby's life seemed pretty normal. Her father was handsome and kind, and worked as a clerk in the Gladstone postal outlet. She had a brother called Brett, who was really old—sixteen, in fact. She thought he was wonderful, and every time he'd bring home one of his football friends, she'd plan to marry him. If he brought two friends in one week, it was tricky trying to decide which husband she'd prefer. But on the whole, Brett was pretty useless to her. He was always off doing his own thing, and when he was home he often called her "Squirt." She could tell he thought she didn't matter. If you're sixteen years old, someone who's nine is worse than nothing.

Carlotta also had two uncles and three aunts, a bedroom with mauve ruffled curtains, a six-speed bike, a best friend called Eleanor, and an orange cat named Marmalade. She had all those things. But if you asked her to tell you about her life, she'd just say, "My mom has leukemia."

The reason she knew her mother had leukemia was that she'd overheard her parents talking about it. "Today," said her mother in a whispery voice, "the doctor said I have to have chemotherapy for my leukemia." Carlotta was listening through the heat register and could hear everything—especially the way her mother started to cry with big heaving sobs. "My hair'll fall out," her mother croaked. She had beautiful thick black hair. Her father murmured some quiet, soothing things that Carlotta couldn't hear.

So Carlotta knew that much about the leukemia and the chemotherapy. But that's all she knew.

One day, when her father was in the yard raking the autumn leaves into a big pile, Carlotta went out and asked him what leukemia was. He looked at her hard. A nerve jumped in his cheek.

"Why are you asking about leukemia?"

"Mom's got it."

There was a pause.

"How did you find out?"

"I heard," said Carlotta.

Her father gave her a big hug, a longer one than usual. "Don't worry about it," he said. "I'm sure it's going to be all right." There was something about that hug that worried Carlotta. And he hadn't told her a single thing.

She decided to ask her mother what leukemia was. Her mother was lying down on the living room sofa, when she should have been out in the kitchen getting dinner ready. It was five o'clock.

"What's leukemia?" asked Carlotta, without even saying hi first.

Her mother looked very startled. "How . . . ?" she said. "When . . . ?"

"I heard," said Carlotta. "Last Tuesday."

Her mother shut her eyes for a moment. Finally she said, "It's a sickness, Carlotta. Lots of people have it. It's no big deal. They'll give me some stuff to make me better."

"Which'll make your hair fall out. *All* of it?"

Her mother paused before answering. "Yes," she said. "I think so."

"You'll be *bald?*" Carlotta's eyes were wide, and bluer than usual.

"Yes." A tear squeezed out of her mother's left eye and dribbled down her cheek. "But I'll wear a big bandanna. You won't see my head. You won't even notice. I often wear bandannas." Then she closed her eyes again. "I need to rest now," she said.

Carlotta stomped upstairs. She knew she ought to say something nice to her mother, or maybe kiss her. But she didn't. She was mad.

She went in her room. She didn't exactly slam the door, but she shut it with a pretty firm thwack. She still didn't know anything worth knowing, and there was a hard lump of anger in her chest. Marmalade was lying on her bed, so she picked him up and hugged him. But even that didn't make her feel better.

Why was her mother sick? She'd kept telling them all to get lots of exercise. She also handed out vitamins, and served lots of milk and whole wheat bread and fruit to make the whole family stay healthy. But did her mom do all those things and eat all that stuff? Carlotta had never noticed whether she did or she didn't. She certainly wasn't healthy, so it must be all her own fault. How could she not practise what she preached? It wasn't fair. There was an apple on her bureau and Carlotta picked it up and threw it in the waste basket. Then she dug a big soggy chocolate bar out of her desk drawer. Her mother wasn't the only one who could break the rules. And since her mother was obviously not going to cook any dinner that night, she'd better eat *something*.

Later, they had pizza for supper. A boy came and delivered it at half past six. Carlotta hated pizza.

At eight o'clock, Carlotta went upstairs and knocked on Brett's door. He was listening to some loud music that Carlotta pretended to like but didn't. "Come in!" he shouted.

"What's leukemia?" she yelled. She yelled so loud that he heard her above the electric guitars and crashing cymbals and drums. He turned off his sound system.

"C'mere," he said. He was sitting on the floor. She went and sat beside him. This made her very nervous. He'd never asked her to sit beside him before. Never. "Look,

Squirt," he said, putting his arm around her shoulder. This made her even more uneasy. "It's okay. It's gonna be just fine. You're too young to worry about junk like that." He gave her a friendly little punch on the same shoulder. "Go to bed," he said. "Get your beauty sleep."

Junk! What she wanted to know was certainly not *junk*.

Later, Carlotta's dad came up and kissed her goodnight and tucked her in.

That's what Mom always used to do.

"Where's Mom?" asked Carlotta.

"She went to bed early," he said. "She's not feeling too perky tonight."

Then he added, "You can't expect parents to be strong and cheerful *all* the time, you know."

Why not? thought Carlotta. *That's what parents are for.* She turned over and pretended she'd fallen asleep. She even concocted a gentle, deep little snore.

The next day in school, Carlotta met Eleanor at the swing set during recess.

"What's leukemia?" said Carlotta.

"Why?" said Eleanor. "Who's got it?"

"Mom," said Carlotta.

"Oh," said Eleanor. There was a long silence.

"*Well?*" urged Carlotta.

Eleanor sighed. "It's a kind of sickness, I guess. Maybe like a cold or the flu or something. I dunno. Ask your dad."

It was Carlotta's turn to sigh. "I did," she said. Her throat was suddenly tight, and she was afraid she might cry or yell or throw something at somebody. She ran back to the school entrance and went in. *I'll hide in the class-room until recess is over.* She felt like she was going to burst wide open, and she didn't want to do it in front of the whole school.

But her teacher, Miss Cassidy, was in her classroom. Carlotta didn't see her at first, because she was down on her hands and knees behind the desk, picking up about five million paper clips she'd dropped. Miss Cassidy was young, with red fly-away hair and a big smile. She wasn't a very serious-looking teacher. By the time she stood up, Carlotta was at her seat, with her face down on the desk, hidden by her arms.

"Carlotta!" Miss Cassidy's voice was worried and kind. "What's wrong?"

Carlotta jumped a bit on her chair. She'd thought she was alone. "Nothing," she said.

Then Miss Cassidy put her hand on her shoulder, very softly. "Tell me," she said.

That did it. Suddenly Carlotta started to cry. She cried hard and out loud, just like the kid next door who was only three years old. She went through the four Kleenexes that Miss Cassidy put in her hand. She felt like she'd never stop crying. But finally she did. About one minute before the bell was due to ring, she was able to speak.

"My mom's got leukemia. No one will tell me what it is. She's tired all the time. Her hair is going to fall out. I'm mad at everybody. I'm even mad at her! *Why won't anyone tell me anything?*"

Miss Cassidy only had time to say one thing before the bell rang and the kids started to pour back into the classroom. "Meet me in the library this afternoon after school's over," she said.

လ

When Carlotta went up to the school library at three o'clock, Miss Cassidy was already sitting at a table with five books piled up beside her. She was running her fingers through her wild hair and taking notes. There were volumes from three encyclopedias, one novel about a young girl with leukemia, and a medical reference book.

"Okay, Carlotta," she said. "Both of us will start searching. I don't know too much about leukemia either, so we can both hunt for answers." She showed Carlotta how to look up the right pages by checking the index and the table of contents. She said, "You start with that book, and I'll start with this one. We'll share what we find out."

A while later, Carlotta said, "Leukemia is a kind of cancer. That's bad. It's not just the flu."

"No, it's not. And yes, it's not good. But I've also just read that some forms of leukemia can be treated very successfully. In this book, it mentions a man who had chemotherapy for his leukemia twenty years ago, and he's still healthy and working at his job."

They read for another half hour or so in silence. Then Carlotta spoke.

"This chemotherapy thing sounds really cool," she said. "But it makes your hair fall out."

"But it grows back," said Miss Cassidy. "And I just learned that it sometimes comes back curly!"

"But you throw up."

"Sometimes, yes. But they have a wonderful new drug that often prevents that."

"Who told you that?" Carlotta was doubtful.

"This medical book. Here, have a look yourself." Miss Cassidy shoved the book across the table.

Carlotta flipped through the pages. She was a fast reader, and could often get the sense of things by just skimming her eyes across the lines of print. She'd already discovered that it wasn't her mother's fault that she was sick. But there were other things to worry her.

"Sometimes people die," Carlotta said. She'd learned this in the very first book she'd opened. Now she felt she was ready to talk about it—*needed* to talk about it. Terrible though the fact was, she had to say it out loud. She had to feel that the fact was out there in the air, instead of squashed inside her head.

"Yes," said Miss Cassidy. "And sometimes they don't."

It felt good to get *that* thought out into the space between Miss Cassidy and herself. Suddenly Carlotta stood up. "It's four-thirty," she said. "I have to be home by five, or Mom gets worried I've been kidnapped or something. Maybe I'll take the novel with me."

Miss Cassidy picked up the other four books and said, "Watch me while I put them back on the shelves. Then you'll know where to find them when you need them."

"Thanks a bunch, Miss Cassidy," said Carlotta, as she put on her jacket. Then she added, "Sorry to use up your Kleenex. But it sure felt good to do all that howling."

"I like to have a little cry myself, from time to time," said Miss Cassidy. "It sort of loosens the kinks. Perhaps you could let your mom do some of that howling."

"Yeah. I know. I already thought of that. And maybe get fond of pizza. Or else learn how to cook something I like. If Mom has a good day tomorrow, I'll ask her to give me a lesson in scrambling eggs. I like eggs. What else? Not broccoli—unless someone says it's a cure for leukemia. Maybe peas. Peas are okay. Or even something spectacular like chocolate pudding."

Miss Cassidy pointed to a shelf in the library. "There are three or four cookbooks over there," she said, "written especially for kids."

"Some place!" said Carlotta as she walked with Miss Cassidy towards the door.

"Right!" laughed Miss Cassidy. Her crazy red hair jiggled up and down. "It's some place, all right!"

༄

As Carlotta walked home, it started to get a bit dark. The sky was a sort of purple colour behind the rooftops, and the bare trees were silhouetted against the sky. She could see how beautiful that was, but she was glad when the street lights suddenly came on, bringing out the late green of the lawns and the bright colours of the painted wooden houses. She could hear the banging and thudding of boxes and machinery down by Halifax Harbour, and she listened to the deep-throated horn of a ship as it moved into sheltered water. She liked those sounds. She hadn't noticed or heard these things for a long time. She'd been shut up inside herself, with her own thoughts and fears keeping everything else out.

Carlotta realized that in some ways nothing had changed. Her mother was still very ill, and nobody at home wanted to talk about it. But even if they didn't, she knew exactly where she could go for help—for a lot of things, not just for information about leukemia. She wasn't sure exactly how to describe what she was feeling, but the word that jumped into her mind was *free*. It was as though some sort of door had opened, and she was able to go through it. On this particular day, that was enough for Carlotta.

Mothers

Sunday, March 23rd

Yesterday I got to be eleven. For my birthday, my mom gave me a diary. It's white with gold letters on it that say *Diary*. It has a little gold metal part (not real gold, I guess) that joins up with a strap so you can snap it shut and lock it. This is to keep prying eyes away from what's inside. Mom said she couldn't have survived adolescence without a diary. She said she wrote down all her stresses and anxieties, and defused herself. *Defused* is a pretty weird word, but then you should know that I'm in love with words. I saved up my allowance for ten whole weeks so I could buy a dictionary. Of course the family has one, but I wanted one of my own. I keep this fact very secret. My friends would laugh themselves sick if they knew about it. But about *defused*. I asked Mom how she spelled it and what it meant. She said that if you remove the explosive part of a bomb, you defuse it. If adolescence is as unbearably painful as everyone says (and on teen TV shows everyone does seem to be disappointed in love or else is being sent to the principal's office or is having babies before they should), I guess it's a good idea to learn as fast as I can how to defuse myself.

Eleven isn't exactly adolescence, but it's a lot older than ten. I can feel the difference already. For one thing, it's got two real digits, not just a one and a zero. And I can sense that I'm marching forward to a THEN that's a whole lot more interesting than the NOW. My sister is fourteen and thinks she's going on nineteen, so you can see why I'm so tired of being young.

Monday, March 24th

I won't tell Mom, but this diary is no good. It's only got these stupid little sections for each day. I'm already in the April 7 slot and I've hardly started. I'll just fill it up and then go out and buy myself a big blank book with limitless space in it.

What did Mom think? That I had nothing to say yet? Did she think that I just wanted to get my feet a little bit wet? She must have thought I didn't know how to write.

But I *do* know how to write. Miss Henson, who's our homeroom teacher, is a big believer in self-expression—in writing and in art. She's making writers of all of us. She says she'd push music and dancing too, except that she's tone deaf and uncoordinated.

Miss Henson also teaches us how to paint wild pictures of things like anger or fear, with just lines and colours. You have to do it with *no objects* in it. I did one of "hate" last week It was supposed to be just a kind of disembodied hate, which is pretty hard to draw. But when I thought about what I'd like to do to Angela Darwin, it was easy to make the picture. I just imagined what it would feel like to slap, slap, *slap* her till her teeth fell out, and then finish it off with a high kick to the stomach. The picture was mostly in reds and blacks, with really strong jagged lines. Miss Henson told me it was good, but when I told her how I did it, she didn't look quite as thrilled as she had before, when she was just looking at the picture.

I thought she was a "New Woman" and would understand. When our parents were little, girls were supposed to be quiet and sweet, but I thought that those things had all changed, and that we were encouraged to assert ourselves. And that it wasn't only boys who could thump around and slam doors (although of course my mother never suggested any such thing, in spite of her interest in the defusing qualities of diaries).

Needless to say, I didn't tell Miss Henson exactly *who* I hated, or even that it was a girl. I just said, "This person." Now I bet she'll be watching me *every minute* to see if she can tell who "this person" is. But she can look forever and not find out. Because Angela Darwin isn't in our school. She's in my gymnastics class down at the Y—*every day* after school. That means I have to face the horrible stuff that she dishes out five times a week.

Angela's not as good as I am on the balance beam and the uneven bars, and she *can't stand* that. Also, most of the kids really like me, and they don't like her. Which makes me safe. Or almost safe. Or maybe, now that I think about it, especially *unsafe*. She's said so many bad things about me (that I'm stingy, conceited, show-offy, ugly) that I think Judy Logan has started to believe some of it. But that doesn't worry me much yet, because I'm not all that crazy about Judy.

But Angela tries to distract me when I'm on the balance beam, and I really mind that. She'll do a sudden big sneeze (fake), or break into fits of the shrieking giggles, just when I'm doing a really tricky move. A couple of times I've missed my footing and fallen right off. Other times I just can't keep the smoothness in my movements. If she wants to beat me at gymnastics, why doesn't she just practise till she gets better, instead of going at everything sideways? And I don't like all that whispering she does behind her hand.

(To be continued.)

Tuesday, March 25th

I go to gymnastics every day because I'm extra good at it and got picked for a special gymnastics club. It's okay to say that in a diary, because no one sees it but me. If I just *said* it, like *out loud*, I'd sound just as conceited as Angela says I am.

Mom loves me being in the gymnastics club and being so good. She's an ambitious mother. I don't like that, because I'd like to do gymnastics just for the fun and joy of it. But the awful thing is that the ambitious mother business starts to rub off on you. You start wanting to be better than everyone else, and to win every ribbon and medal in sight.

Mom wants me to get high marks, too. And to be pretty. She's really a nice mother—much nicer than a lot of mothers I know who are crabby, and even yell a lot at their kids. But I hate that ambition stuff. She makes me feel like a horse that she's grooming for some large event, some large *equestrian* event. I don't think she'll stop loving me if I turn out to be clumsy and dumb and ugly, but sometimes I feel like I'd just love to goof off and walk around Point Pleasant Park all by myself until the knots let go of my chest. I want them to untie and sort of lie inside me like a pile of loose string.

Point Pleasant Park is—uh, oh. Mom's calling out to me that my light should have been out an hour ago.

Wednesday, March 26th

Well, I sure ran at the mouth last night. By the time I turned out my light it was ten-thirty. And I hadn't even started my math homework. I *detest* math. I don't mind the regular stuff, but I hate what the teacher calls "problems"— like: If a man can walk three miles in two hours, how long does it take him to walk seven miles? Now that one's easy. Even I can figure that one out (I think), but mostly, as soon as I start even *reading* the problem, I can feel my brain freezing up and refusing even to think. With a frozen brain you can't think anyway. All that grey stuff in there is stiff and unusable. Sometimes the same thing happens with trying to remember *le* and *la* in French. What does it matter, anyway? A chair's a chair. Who cares if it's a she-chair or a he-chair? *La chaise.* The reason I know that is that my brain unfroze long enough for me to imagine a flounce around the four sides of the chair. Same thing with a table. *La table.* The French teacher says that after a while the right articles (*le* and *la, un* and *une*) just *sound* right. When? How soon? I'm waiting.

I have to do my math. Miss Henson was kind of mad at me today. No, she was disappointed. That's far worse. She said, "Writing all those pages in your diary is no excuse. You're good at writing, and I'm glad about that. But later on in your life, it's not going to be any use at all to be able to write stories and poems if you can't also figure out your bank statement or do your income tax calculations. Your sister Barbara *liked* math." I was sort of surprised and shocked. I thought about those hours and hours of talk about freeing ourselves to create, and all the time what Miss Henson had been thinking about was *money*. And I didn't want to hear about Barbara and her love affair with math.

I'll tell you about Point Pleasant Park as soon as I can. No time right now. I have *twelve* problems to do. Six from yesterday and six more for today. Crime doesn't pay.

Friday, March 28th

No time to write in my diary yesterday. More math problems. Point Pleasant Park is on a giant piece of land—acres and acres of it—at the south end of Halifax. There are lots of paths and some old forts, and more trees than anyone could ever count. But I'm not a million percent crazy about trees. I mean, I like trees and all that, but I don't want to be closed in by thousands of them. I love the part of the park that's by the sea. Because it's open, with lots of sky. You can see the big boats coming and going, and watch the ducks and seagulls and sandpipers. They make me feel free, like I had wings, too.

But Mom says I mustn't go there alone. She says a man might find me and do something bad to me. That's all she says, but I know what she means. She means a man might kidnap me, or knock me down for my money, or rape me. No one's going to kidnap me. My dad doesn't have enough money to make it worthwhile for a man to drag me (biting, kicking, screaming blue murder) out the park gates to wherever he hides his truck or car.

And knock me down for my money? What money? I keep my allowance at home in a Pot o' Gold chocolate box. Every week Dad brings Mom a box of those chocolates. He hands them over with a kind of flourish, and I guess she's supposed to act deeply grateful, which she never does. Of course not. They're really a present to himself. She'd rather have a box of licorice whips or a bag of chocolate brooms. Dad says that no one who's thirty-nine years old should eat such garbage. But he sits up there in the den, watching the ten o'clock news, eating all the chocolates with soft centres. Us kids get to eat the nougats and nuts and caramels, and Mom just picks out the bordeaux chocolates. Then she never eats another single one.

Oh yes, the man in the park could also rape me. What? Rape *me?* I'm eleven years old and have pigtails and bands on my teeth. I really don't think this could possibly be a problem. You must wonder how I know what rape is. It's not like it's something that happens any old day in the Saint Francis School yard, beside the jungle gym.

But I know what it is. I read about it in Ginny's book about babies and sex and stuff. Rape is when a man puts his thing into your hole (the one that's for that purpose, which is also the one that babies come out of. Much to my surprise. I would have thought that the belly button was a more sensible—and cleaner—location) without your consent. *Consent* means agreeing that it's okay. (Miss Henson says I'm good with words. She's right, I guess. I collect them like some people collect stamps, and write the really delicious ones in a book.) Of course I wouldn't give my consent for any such thing. In fact, I can't imagine it being enjoyable *at all*, even with my husband. But Ginny's mother told her that when you're ready for it, it's nice. Even fun. She didn't go on to explain about when you could expect to be ready.

I did okay on my math, yesterday. Miss Henson was pleased.

Monday, March 31st

I have awful news. Angela Darwin's family is moving and she's going to be in my school district. This is a high-power, four-star, full-fledged disaster. Miss Henson will see hate radiating off me in waves. She'll know right away whose front teeth I wish I could knock out.

We had a spelling bee today, and I got to be a captain. We had six on our team, including Wayne McKeigan. What a sharp name, eh? Anyway, we won, and we all hugged each other and yelled. Wayne McKeigan hugged me. Then he looked at me and turned beet red, and ran out of the gym. I thought that was pretty weird. Well, we're both good spellers. I guess it's not a love affair. Ginny's book says you don't get interested in boys until you're twelve. Then you have your period (maybe then, maybe earlier or later) and grow breasts. But I'll tell you something, Diary. I'm interested in boys *right now*. Maybe I'm a freak. I like looking at Wayne McKeigan's freckles and the way he skims around the gym when we play dodge ball. It's like a kind of dance. I like well-coordinated athletic people. But I don't hold it against Miss Henson that she's got two left feet.

It's good to have a diary so you can say all these things out loud. I'd die before I'd say things like that to my mother—or even to Ginny.

Tuesday, April 1st

Angela Darwin came to school for the first time today. I watched while the principal handed her over to Miss

Henson, and the way Miss Henson was smiling and saying nice things to Angela and putting her hand on her shoulder. Angela was being all full of sweetness and politeness, and I wanted to yell, "Watch out, everybody! This kid's a walking vial of deadly poison!"

I took a good hard look at her while all the good cheer was going on at the front of the room. She's pretty. I hadn't really noticed that before, but she is. Unfortunately. She's got dark blond wavy hair and sort of creamy skin and brown eyes. Blonds often have pinkish raw-looking skin that gets a sunburn if it's out in the sun for more than two seconds. Not Angela. She'll be so beautiful in July that I'll abhor her even harder than I do now. Tanned skin is much more gorgeous than white skin. Real black people have such beautiful skin that it's all I can do to keep from asking them if I can touch it.

At recess I went over to Angela and gave her my own warm and tender smile. "Hope you like it here at Saint Francis," I said. No point in sticking out my neck so that she can cut off my head on the very first day. Then I sort of stuck around. If she was going to start telling my friends that I was stingy, conceited, show-offy and ugly, I wanted to be the first one to hear it.

But she didn't. Not today, anyway, even though it's April Fool's Day.

Friday, April 4th

We have a bunch of exams next week. I can't write in

my diary till they're all over. Mom is starting to poke her
nose in my room in the evenings, to see if I've done my
studying. This week there'll be a lot of snooping around.
Last week she said, "Well, you led the class last term. I
don't see why you can't do it again." I wish she wouldn't
do that.

Tonight she looked at me and said, "Let's see if we can
do something with that hair."

"What hair?" I growled.

"*Your* hair, of course, silly!" She was smiling, very
friendly and loving, but I could feel the grooming thing
about to happen again.

"What's *wrong* with my hair?" I said.

"Well, nothing, really," she said. "But wouldn't it be
fun to try curling it? Just on the ends? And maybe wear it
loose, for once."

"Mom," I said, "I do gymnastics every day. What am I
going to do with all that hair flying around? Even the
pigtails get in the way."

"Tomorrow's Saturday," she said. "No gymnastics."

"Okay, okay," I muttered, but I felt really mad. Like it
wasn't my own head or hair. Like I didn't have control
over my own body.

Which, of course, I don't.

Saturday, April 5th

Like I said, I can't write in my diary for a week, but I
need to say just one thing.

Mom put my hair up in curlers last night. I felt like I was sleeping on rocks. In the morning she brushed it out *(ouch!)* and then combed it very carefully.

"It looks beautiful," she said. "It may be an uninteresting colour, but the texture is lovely."

Uninteresting colour? I thought about Angela's blond waves and gritted my teeth.

"What do you mean, *uninteresting colour?*" I asked. Not very sweetly, either.

"Well," she said. "You know. Just *brown.*" Hers is a deep red—auburn is the right word—and thick. My sister's is almost jet black and very dramatic against her pale and flawless skin. Lucky Barbara.

I went to the store in my new hair. I didn't want to like it, but I sort of did. I walked along and enjoyed the way it went flip-flip with each step I took. I tossed my head, and it swept over my left shoulder.

At the store I came face to face with Angela. She looked at me and burst out laughing. "Trying to look like a glamour girl?" she said. "Better wait till you get those bands off your teeth. Find something better to do with your time."

On the way home, I thought about how the Darwins had only been in their house for six days. I guess I can't expect them to move out again next week. Angela's installed in it, and I'm going to be stuck with her for a long time.

When I got home, I looked at myself in the mirror. Nose okay. Eyes pretty good—blue with brown flecks—but I think I need glasses. Mouth. I smiled. A row of stainless steel flashed back at me. Skin? Okay, but no big deal. You're right, Angela. Not much to work with there. My mother's ambitions in the beauty department are doomed. I pulled my hair back into a ponytail, stuck my tongue out at the mirror, and left the bathroom.

So—I'd better start studying for my French and math tests. If I can't be beautiful, I'd better try for a brilliant mind.

Monday, April 14th

The exams are over. Ginny came first. Wayne came second. I came third. Angela came fifteenth. I counted down the list, feeling exactly like my mother as I did it. People say daughters often end up being carbon copies of their mothers. I'm hoping that you can escape that fate if you really try.

When I have kids, I'm not going to make a wild, ridiculous fuss about all their successes (like learning to tie shoelaces or reciting their ABCs or getting prizes at school) except for saying in a gentle kind of way, "Oh, good for you." And I'll never say, "Come on. Pull up your socks and see if you can beat Harriet (or Jim or Sally or George) in the math exam (or the skating competition or the public speaking contest or the spelling bee)." Then my kids will feel so deprived because of my lack of interest that they'll vow to be really pushy with their own kids. It seems to me that this is what happens in real history. People keep see-sawing back and forth between wars and reforms and wars and reforms. But as far as I can see, no one ever really learns much of anything.

I rushed home from school and yelled, "Hey, Mom! Guess what? I came third in the class!"

"Who came first?" That's what she said.

"Ginny," I mumbled, all the steam gone out of my engine. Then I ran upstairs and slammed my bedroom door.

I could hear my parents downstairs. Their voices come up the hot-air register as clear as if they were on the telephone. You can't believe the secrets I've discovered just by lying on my bed beside that register. I could hear my mother speaking,

"Now what on earth is wrong with *her?*" she said. "Why all the slamming?"

"Maybe you could have said, 'Good for you,'" said my father. My mother's very *dominant,* and I think he's a little bit scared of crossing her path. He's not exactly *passive,* and he's certainly not *recessive* (that's for genes), but he doesn't push himself around much either. So I was grateful that he came to my assistance.

"Well," said Mom, "she's really smart, and I know she could do better. So why not say so? She's always staring off into space, or reading trashy kid novels, or else writing in that diary I was stupid enough to give her. Why don't *you* ever push her a little?"

He must have eaten a whole lot of that new "Müesli" cereal for breakfast that day, because he was sounding very strong and sure. "Because I think coming third is fine. Why does it have to be first? I never came first in my class, not even once, and I can't see that it's wrecked my life. I have a good job, and a pretty wife and two daughters who like me, and a nice little house. Also a canoe and a lot of fishing equipment. I'm not looking for the Nobel Prize."

I could hear my mother chuckle. "Maybe the Peace Prize," she said, and I could hear a sort of rustly silence like they might be hugging or something.

My dad is a lawyer. Not a big fancy money-making lawyer, but a quiet and happy one. Because of the recession, people sometimes pay him with eggs or apples or even once a skinny-looking chicken. No one's ever going to make him a judge, because he likes doing exactly what he's doing. He told me that once. Mom went to university and got really high marks. People thought she'd set the world on fire and would end up the first woman prime minister or something. But she didn't. She had babies and just did the mother thing. When Barbara and I got to be older (about eight and five) she wanted to get a job, but by then there were no jobs for her. There's a grudging part of me that understands why Mom wants me to get to be something she always wanted to be but never was. But I hope I don't do that to my kids. I'm me, and she's her.

Mom's not a monster, you know, Diary. She hugs us all a lot—even Barbara—and really loves us. I guess I just want her to be perfect. Like she wants *me* to be perfect.

I wrote so much tonight because we have a holiday next week, so I can stay up late. Also, I felt I needed very badly to defuse myself.

Thursday, April 24th

Today I had to take a geography book and an atlas over to Angela's house. She wasn't in school and we have a geography test next Thursday. Miss Henson found the books on the old cupboard behind her desk. She said to me, "Better take these to Angela on your way home. If she has that flu that's going around, she may be away for several days." She also told me some stuff to tell Angela about our math homework.

I was in a hurry after school, because it takes a half hour to walk to the Y, and I had gymnastics at four. So I almost ran to the Darwins' house. Mrs. Darwin answered the door. She's a blond like Angela and has lots of curls, too (not just waves), but the colour of her hair is kind of yellow and dry looking. I guess she's what my mother calls a "bottle blond."

I said, "Can I see Angela, Mrs. Darwin? I've got stuff from school and I need to explain it to her."

She looked kind of wild and frantic, and I wondered what was wrong. She said, "No. You can't see her. She's too sick. She's in bed, and you might catch it. It might be scarlet fever." I shoved the books into her hands and started to back out the door. Sometimes people die with scarlet fever. I sure didn't want to catch it. Especially not from Angela.

Then I looked up, and Angela was coming down the stairs. She didn't have her pyjamas or nightie on or anything, just the usual stuff she wears in the daytime.

Mrs. Darwin could see that I was looking at something, and she swung around to see what it was. Then she started to yell at Angela, almost scream at her.

"Get back up there! Don't you *dare* come downstairs!"

But Angela kept coming. She was staring straight ahead and walking like some kind of wind-up toy. She looked like she was in some sort of trance. And as she got closer, I saw that her face was all swollen on one side, especially under the eye, and that it was red and sort of blue around that corner of her mouth.

Her mother rushed over and grabbed her by the arm (not the hand, the *arm*) and dragged her over to the kitchen and shoved her in, slamming the door behind her. She pulled her like she was a bag of bricks or something. Just before she closed the door, I could hear Mrs. Darwin hiss at her, *"I'll get you for this!"*

When she turned around, she was smiling with her red lips and cold eyes, and saying, "She was upset this morning and walked into a door."

Now it was my turn to act like I was in a trance. "Tell her to do pages 19 to 23 in her math book," I said, "and the geography test is on Thursday." Then I turned around and walked down the front steps, trying to keep myself from running, which is what I really wanted to do. When I turned the corner, I ran home and raced upstairs and shut the door of my room behind me. I forgot all about going to gymnastics.

Tonight I'm lying here thinking about how I was able to draw that picture of hate because I was thinking about slap, slap slapping Angela Darwin. I'm feeling a whole bunch of things right now, but they're all jumbled up, and I don't know how to sort any of them out. I sure could do with a whole lot of defusing tonight.

The Metaphor

Miss Hancock was plump and unmarried and over-enthusiastic. She was fond of peasant blouses encrusted with embroidery, from which loose threads invariably dangled. Like a heavy bird, she fluttered and flitted from desk to desk, inspecting notebooks, making suggestions, dispensing eager praise. Miss Hancock was our teacher of literature and creative writing.

If one tired of scrutinizing Miss Hancock's clothes, which were nearly always as flamboyant as her nature, one could still contemplate her face with considerable satisfaction. It was clear that this was a face that had once been pretty, although cloakroom discussions of her age never resulted in any firm conclusions. In any case, by now it was too late for simple, unadorned prettiness. What time had taken away from her, Miss Hancock tried to replace by artificial means, and she applied her makeup with an excess of zeal and a minimum of control. Her face was truly amazing. She was fond of luminous frosted lipsticks—in hot pink, or something closer to purple or magenta. Her eyelashes curled up and out singly, like a row of tiny bent sticks. Surrounding her eyes, the modulations of colour, toners, shadows could keep a student interested for half an hour if he or she were bored with a grammar assignment. Her head was covered with a profusion of small busy curls, which were brightly, aggressively golden—"in bad taste," my mother said, "like the rest of her."

However, do not misunderstand me. We were fond of Miss Hancock. In fact, almost to a person, we loved her. Our class, like most groups that are together for long periods of time, had developed a definite personality. By some fluke of geography or biology or school administration, ours was a cohesive group composed of remarkably backward grade seven pupils—backward in that we had not yet embraced sophistication, boredom, cruelty, drugs, alcohol, or sex. Those who didn't fit into our mould were in the minority and made little mark upon us. We were free to respond positively to Miss Hancock's literary excesses without fear of the mockery of our peers, and with an open and uninhibited delight that is often hard to find in any classroom above the level of grade five. So Miss Hancock was able to survive, even to flourish, in our unique, sheltered environment.

Miss Hancock was equally at home in her two fields of creative writing and literature. It was the first time I had been excited, genuinely moved, by poems, plays, stories. She could analyze without destroying a piece of literature, and we argued about meanings and methods and creative intentions with passionate caring. She had a beautiful deeply modulated voice, and when she read poetry aloud, we sat bewitched, transformed. We could not have said which we loved best, Miss Hancock or her subject. They were all of a piece.

But it was in the area of composition, in her creative writing class, that Miss Hancock made the deepest mark upon me. She had that gift of making most of us want to write, to communicate, to make a blank sheet of paper into a beautiful or at least an interesting thing. We were as drugged by words as some children are by electronic games.

One October day, just after Thanksgiving, Miss Hancock came into the classroom and faced us, eyes aglitter, hands clasped in front of her embroidered breasts.

"Today," she announced, clapping her dimpled hands together, her charm bracelets jingling, "we are going to do a lovely exercise. Such *fun!*" She lifted her astonishing eyes to the classroom ceiling. "A whole new world of composition is about to open for you in one glorious *whoosh.*" She stood there, arms now raised, elbows bent, palms facing us, enjoying her dramatic pause. "After today," she announced in a loud confidential whisper, "you will have a brand new weapon in your arsenal of writing skills. You will possess . . . (pause again) The Metaphor!" Her arms fell, and she clicked to the blackboard in her patent-leather pumps to start the lesson. Her dazzling curls shone in the afternoon sunlight and jiggled as she wrote. Then, with a board full of examples and suggestions, she began her impassioned discourse on The Metaphor. I listened, entranced. Miss Hancock may have been in poor taste, but at that time in my life she was my entry to something I did not yet fully understand but that I knew I wanted.

"And now," Miss Hancock announced, after the lucid and fervent presentation of her subject, "The Metaphor is yours—to *use*, to *enjoy*, to *relish*." She stood poised, savouring one of her breathless pauses. "I now want you to take out your notebooks," she continued, "and make a list. Write down the members of your family, your home, your pets, anything about which you feel *deeply*. Then," she went on, "I want you to describe everyone and everything on your list with a pungent and a telling metaphor." She gave a little clap. "Now *start!*" she cried. She sat down at her desk, clasping her hands together so tightly that the knuckles looked polished. Smiling tensely, frilled eyes shining, she waited.

All but the dullest of us were excited. This was an unfamiliar way of looking at things. Better still, it was a brand new method of talking about them.

Miss Hancock interrupted us just one more time. "Write quickly," she urged from her glowing, expectant position at the desk. "Don't think too hard. Let your writing, your words, emerge from you like a mysterious and elegant blossom. Let it all *out*"—she closed her lacy eyes—"without restraint, without inhibition, with *verve*."

Well, we did. The results, when we read them out to her, were, as one might expect, hackneyed, undistinguished, ordinary. But we were delighted with ourselves. And she with us. She wrote our metaphors on the blackboard and expressed her pleasure with small, delighted gasping sounds.

"My dog is a clown in a spotted suit."

"My little brother George is a whirling top."

"The spruce tree was a tall lady in a stiff dress."

"My dad is a warm wood stove."

And so it went. Finally it was my turn. I offered metaphors for my father, my grandmother, my best friend, the waves at Peggy's Cove. Then I looked at the metaphor for my mother. I hadn't realized I had written so much.

"Miss Hancock," I hesitated, "the one for my mother is awfully long. You probably don't want to write all this stuff down."

"Oh, *heavens*, Charlotte," breathed Miss Hancock, "of *course* I want it! Read it all to us. Do, Charlotte. Oh, *do!*"

I began: "My mother is a flawless modern building, created of glass and the smoothest of pale concrete. Inside are business offices furnished with beige carpets and gleaming chrome. In every room there are machines— recording devices, fax machines, copiers, computers. They are buzzing and clicking away, absorbing and spitting out information with a speed and skill that is not normal. Downstairs, at ground level, people walk in and out, tracking mud and dirt over the steel-grey tiles, marring the cool perfection of the building. There are no comfortable chairs in the lobby."

I sat down, eyes on my desk. There was a pause so long that I finally felt forced to look up. Miss Hancock was standing there at the front of the room, chalk poised, perfectly still. Then she turned around quickly and wrote the whole metaphor verbatim (verbatim!) on the board. When she faced us again, she looked normal once more. Smiling brightly, she said, "Very, *very* good, class! I had planned to discuss with you what you all *meant* by your metaphors; I had hoped to probe their *significance*. But I have to leave early today because of a dental appointment." Then, with five vigorous sweeps of her blackboard eraser, the whole enticing parade of metaphors disappeared from the board, leaving us feeling vaguely deprived. It also left me feeling more than vaguely relieved. "Class dismissed!" said Miss Hancock cheerily, and then, "Charlotte. May I see you for a moment before you go?"

When the others had gathered up their books and their leftover lunches, they disappeared into the corridor. I went up to the front of the room to Miss Hancock's desk. She was sitting there soberly, hands still, eyes quiet.

"Yes, Miss Hancock?" I inquired, mystified.

"Charlotte," she began, "your metaphors were unusually good, unusually interesting. For someone your age, you have quite a complex vocabulary, a truly promising way of expressing yourself."

Ah. So this was why she wanted to see me. But apparently it was not.

"I wonder," she continued slowly, carefully, "do you have anything you would like to discuss about your mother's metaphor?"

I thought about that.

"No," I replied. "I don't think so. I don't really know what it means. It just sort of came out. I feel kind of funny about it."

"Lots of things just sort of come out when you're writing," said Miss Hancock quietly, oh so quietly, as though she were afraid something fragile might break if she spoke too quickly, too loudly. "And there's no need to feel funny about it. I don't want to push you even a little bit, but are you really sure you don't want to discuss it?" I could tell that she was feeling concerned and kind, not nosy.

"Lookit," I said, using an expression that my mother particularly disliked, "that's really nice of you, but I can't think of anything at all to say. Besides, even though you say there's no need to feel funny, I really do feel sort of creepy about it. And I'm not all that crazy about the feeling." I paused, not sure of what else to say.

Miss Hancock was suddenly her old self again. "*Well!*" she said cheerfully, as she rose. "That's perfectly fine. I just wanted you to know that your writing was very intriguing today and that it showed a certain maturity that surprised and delighted me." She gathered up her books, her purse, her pink angora cardigan, and started off toward the corridor. At the door, she stopped and turned around, solemn and quiet once more. "Charlotte," she

said, "if you ever need any help—with your writing, or,
well, with any other kind of problem—just let me know."
Then she turned abruptly and clicked off in the direction
of the staff room, waving her hand in a fluttery farewell.
"My dental appointment," she called merrily.

I walked home slowly, hugging my books to my chest.
The mid-October sun shone down upon the coloured
leaves that littered the sidewalk, and I kicked and shuffled
as I walked, enjoying the swish and scrunch, savouring the
sad-sweet feeling of doom that October always gives me.
I thought for a while about my metaphor—the one Miss
Hancock had asked about—and then I decided to push it
out of my head.

When I arrived home, I opened the door with my key,
entered the front porch, took off my shoes, and read the
note on the hall table. It was written in flawless script on
a small piece of bond paper. It said: "At a Children's Aid
board meeting. Home by 5. Please tidy your room."

The hall table was polished, antique, perfect. It contained
one silver salver for messages and a small ebony lamp with
a white shade. The floor of the entrance hall was tiled. The
black and white tiles shone in the sunlight, unmarked by
any sign of human contact. I walked over them carefully,
slowly, having slipped and fallen once too often.

Hunger. I went into the kitchen and surveyed it
thoughtfully. More black and white tiles dazzled the eye,
and the cupboards and walls were a blinding spotless
white. The counters shone, empty of jars, leftovers, canis-
ters, appliances. The whole room looked as though it were

waiting for the movers to arrive with the furniture and dishes. I made myself a peanut butter sandwich, washed the knife and plate, and put everything away. Then I went upstairs to my room, walking up the grey stair carpet beside the off-white walls, glancing absently at the single lithograph in its black frame. "My home," I said aloud, "is a box. It is cool and quiet and empty and uninteresting. Nobody lives in the box." Entering my room, I looked around. A few magazines were piled on the floor beside my bed. On my dresser, a T-shirt lay on top of my ivory brush and comb set. Two or three books were scattered over the top of my desk. I picked up the magazines, removed the T-shirt, and put the books back in the bookcase. There. Done.

Then I called Julia Parsons, who was my best friend, and went over to her house to talk about boys. When I returned at six o'clock, my mother, who had been home only one hour, had prepared a complicated three-course meal—expert, delicious, nutritious. "There's food in the box," I mused.

Since no one else had much to say at dinner, I talked about school. I told them about Miss Hancock's lesson on The Metaphor. I said what a marvellous teacher she was, how even the dumbest of us had learned to enjoy writing compositions, how she could make the poetry in our textbook so exciting to read and to hear.

My father listened attentively, enjoying my enthusiasm. He was not a lively or an original man, but he was an intelligent person who liked to watch eagerness in others. "You're very fortunate, Charlotte," he said, "to find a teacher who can wake you up and make you love literature."

"Is she that brassy Miss Hancock whom I met at the home and school meeting?" asked my mother.

"What do you mean, brassy?"

"Oh. You know. Overdone, too much enthusiasm. Flamboyant. Orange hair. Is she the one?"

"Yes," I said.

"Oh," said my mother, without emphasis of any kind. "Her. Charlotte, would you please remove the dishes and bring in the dessert. Snow pudding. In the fridge, top left-hand side. Thank you."

That night I lay in the bath among the Estée Lauder bubbles (gift from my father on my last birthday) and created metaphors. I loved baths. The only thing nicer than one bath a day was two. Julia said that if I kept taking so many baths, my skin would get dry and crisp, and that I'd be wrinkled before I was thirty. That was too far away to worry about. She also said that taking baths was disgusting and that showers were more hygienic. She pointed out that I was soaking in my own dirt, like bathers in the fetid Ganges. I thought this a bit excessive and said so. "For pete's sake!" I exclaimed. "If I have two baths a day, I can't be sitting in very much dirt. Besides, it's *therapeutic*."

"It's *what?*"

"Therapeutic. Water play. I read about it in *Reader's Digest* at the doctor's office. They let kids play with water when they're wild and upset. And now they're using warm baths to soothe the patients in mental hospitals."

"So?"

"So it could be useful if I happen to end up crazy." I laughed. I figured that would stop her. It did.

In the bath I always did a lot of things besides wash. I lifted up mounds of the tiny bubbles and held them against the fluorescent light over the sink. The patterns and shapes were delicate, like minute filaments of finest lace. I poked my toes through the bubbles and waved their hot pinkness to and fro among the static white waves. I hopefully examined my breasts for signs of sudden growth. If I lay down in the tub and brought the bubbles up over my body and squeezed my chest together by pressing my arms inward, I could convince myself that I was full-breasted and seductive. I did exercises to lengthen my hamstrings, in order to improve my splits for the gymnastics team. I thought about Charles Swinimer. I quoted poetry out loud with excessive feeling and dramatic emphasis, waving my soapy arms around and pressing my eloquent hand against my flat chest. And from now on, I also lay there and made up metaphors, most of them about my mother.

"My mother is a white picket fence—straight, level. The fence stands in a field full of weeds. The field is bounded on all sides by thorny bushes and barbed wire."

"My mother is a lofty mountain capped by virgin snow. The air around the mountain is clear and clean and very cold." I turned on more hot water. "At the base of the mountain grow gnarled and crooked trees, surrounded by scrub brush and poison ivy."

Upon leaving the bath, I would feel no wiser. Then I would clean the tub very carefully indeed. It was necessary.

Not, mind you, that my mother ranted and raved about her cleanliness. Ranting and raving were not part of her style. "I know you will agree," she would say ever so sweetly, implying in some oblique way that I certainly did not agree, "that it is an inconsiderate and really ugly thing to leave a dirty tub." Then she would lead me with a subtle soft-firm pressure into the bathroom so that we might inspect together a bathtub ringed with sludge, sprinkled with hair and dried suds. "Not," she would say quietly, "a very pretty sight."

And what, I would ask myself, is so terrible about that? Other mothers—I knew, I had heard them—nagged, yelled, scolded, did terrible and noisy things. But what was it about my mother's methods that left me feeling so depraved, so unsalvageable?

But of course I was thirteen by now, and knew all about cleaning tubs and wiping off countertops and sweeping up crumbs. A very small child must have been a terrible test to that cool and orderly spirit. I remember those days. A toy ceased to be a toy and began to be a mess the moment it left the toy cupboard. "I'm sure," she would say evenly, "that you don't want to have those blocks all over the carpet. Why not keep them all in one spot, over there behind Daddy's chair?" From time to time I attempted argument.

"But, Mother, I'm making a garden."

"Then make a *little* garden. They're every bit as satisfying as large, sprawling, unmanageable farms."

And since no one who was a truly nice person would want a large, sprawling, unmanageable farm, I would move my blocks behind the chair and make my small garden there. Outside, our backyard was composed of grass and flowers, plus one evergreen tree that dropped neither fuzzy buds in the spring nor ragged leaves in the fall. No swing set made brown spots on that perfect lawn, nor was there a sandbox. Cats were known to use sandboxes as community toilets. Or so my mother told me. I assume she used the term *toilet* (a word not normally part of her vocabulary) instead of washroom, lest there be any confusion as to her meaning.

But in grade seven, you no longer needed a sandbox. My friends marvelled when they came to visit, which wasn't often. How serene my mother seemed, how lovely to look at, with her dark blond hair, her flawless figure, her smooth hands. She never acted frazzled or rushed or angry, and her forehead was unmarked by age or worry lines. Her hair always looked as though a hairdresser had arrived at six o'clock to ready her for the day. "Such a peaceful house," my friends would say, clearly impressed, "and no one arguing or fighting." Then they would leave and go somewhere else for their snacks, their music, their hanging around.

No indeed, I thought. No fights in this house. It would be like trying to down an angel with a BB gun—both sacrilegious and futile. My father, thin and nervous, was careful about hanging up his clothes and keeping his sweaters in neat piles. He certainly didn't fight with my mother. In fact, he said very little at all to her. He had probably learned early that to complain is weak, to rejoice is childish, to laugh is noisy. And moving around raises dust.

This civilized, this clean, this disciplined woman who was and is my mother was also, if one were to believe her admirers, the mainstay of the community, the rock upon which the town was built. She chaired committees, ran bazaars, sat on boards. When I first heard about this, I thought it a very exciting thing that she sat on boards. If my mother, who sat so correctly on the needlepoint chair with her nylon knees pressed so firmly together, could actually sit on *boards,* there might be a rugged and reckless side to her that I had not yet met. The telephone rang constantly, and her softly controlled voice could be heard, hour after hour, arranging and steering and manipulating the affairs of the town.

Perhaps because she juggled her community jobs, her housework, her cooking and her grooming with such quiet, calm efficiency, she felt scorn for those less able to cope. "Mrs. Langstreth says she is too *tired* to take on a table at the bazaar," she might say. It was not hard to visualize Mrs. Langstreth lounging on a sofa, probably in a turquoise chenille dressing gown, surrounded by full ashtrays and neglected children. Or my mother might comment quietly, but with unmistakable emphasis, "Gillian

Munroe is having trouble with her children. And in my opinion, she has only herself to blame." The implication seemed to be that if Gillian Munroe's children were left in my mother's care for a few weeks, she could make them all into a perfectly behaved family. Which was probably true.

Certainly in those days I was well behaved. I spoke quietly, never complained, ate whatever was put before me, and obeyed all rules without question or argument. I was probably not even very unhappy, though I enjoyed weekdays much more than weekends. Weekends didn't yet include parties or boys. It is true that Julia and I spent a lot of our time together talking about boys. I also remember stationing myself on the fence of the vacant lot on Seymour Street at five o'clock, the hour when Charles Swinimer could be expected to return from high school. As he passed, I'd be too absorbed in my own activity to look at him directly. I'd be chipping the bark off the fence, or reading, or pulling petals from a daisy—he loves me, he loves me not. Out of the corner of my eye, I feasted upon his jaw line, his confident walk, his shoulders. On the rare days when he would toss me a careless "Hi" (crumbs to a pigeon), I would have to dig my nails into the wood to keep from falling off, from fainting dead away. But that was the extent of my thrills. No boys had yet materialized in the flesh to offer themselves to me. Whatever else they were looking for, it was not acne, straight, brown stringy hair or measurements of 32-32-32.

So weekdays were still best. Weekdays meant school and particularly English class, where Miss Hancock delivered up feasts of succulent literature for our daily consumption. *Hamlet* was the thing that spring, the spring before we moved into grade eight. So were a number of poems that left me weak and changed. And our composition class gathered force, filling us with a creative confidence that was heady stuff. We wrote short stories, played with similes, created poems that did and did not rhyme, felt we were capable of anything and everything; if Shakespeare, if Wordsworth could do it, why couldn't we? Over it all, Miss Hancock presided, hands fluttering, voice atremble with a raw emotion.

But *Hamlet* dominated our literature classes from April to June. Like all serious students, we agonized and argued over its meaning, Hamlet's true intent, his sanity, his goal. Armed with rulers, we fought the final duel with its bloody sequence, and a five-foot Fortinbras stepped among the dead bodies between the desks to proclaim the ultimate significance of it all. At the end, Miss Hancock stood, hands clasped, knuckles white, tears standing in her eyes. And I cannot pretend that all of ours were dry.

At the close of the year, our class bought an enormous tasteless card of thanks and affixed it to a huge trophy. The trophy was composed of two brass-coloured Ionic pillars that were topped by a near-naked athlete carrying a spiky wreath. On the plate below was inscribed: "For you and Hamlet with love. The grade seven class. 1990."

When my mother saw it, she came close to losing her cool control.

"Who chose it?" she asked, tight-lipped.

"Horace Hannington," I answered. Oh, don't spoil it, don't spoil it.

"That explains it," she said, and mercifully that was all.

ⱷ

Junior high school passed, and so did innocence and acne. Hair curled, makeup intact, I entered high school the year that Charles Swinimer left for university. But there would be other fish to fry. Outwardly blasé, single-minded and sixteen, I came into my first grade ten class with a mixture of intense apprehension and a burning unequivocal belief that high school could and would deliver up to me all of life's most precious gifts—the admiration of my peers, local fame, boys, social triumphs. During August of that year, my family had moved to another school district. I entered high school with a clean slate. It was terrifying to be so alone. I also knew that it was a rare and precious opportunity; I could approach life without being branded with my old failures, my old drawbacks. I was pretty; I had real curves; I was anonymous; I melted into the crowd. No one here would guess that I had once been such a skinny, pimply wretch.

Our first class was geography, and I knew enough of the material to be able to let my eyes and mind wander. Before the end of the period, I knew that the boy to pursue was Howard Oliver, that the most prominent and therefore the most potentially useful or dangerous girl was Gladys Simpson, that geography was uninteresting, that the teacher was strict. To this day I can smell the classroom during that first period—the dry and acrid smell of chalk, the cool, sweet fragrance of the freshly waxed floors, the perspiration that travelled back to me from Joey Elliot's desk.

The next period was English. My new self-centred and self-conscious sophistication had not blunted my love of literature, my desire to write, to play with words, to express my discoveries and confusions. I awaited the arrival of the teacher with masked but real enthusiasm. I was not prepared for the entrance of Miss Hancock.

Miss Hancock's marked success with fifteen years of grade seven students had finally transported her to high places. She entered the classroom, wings spread, ready to fly. She was used to success, and she was eager to sample the pleasure of a group of older and more perceptive minds. Clad in royal blue velour, festooned with gold chains, hair glittering in the sun pouring in from the east window, fringed eyes darting, she faced the class, arms raised. She paused.

"Let us pray!" said a deep male voice from the back row. It was Howard Oliver. Laughter exploded in the room. Behind my Duo-Tang folder, I snickered fiercely.

Miss Hancock's hands fluttered wildly. It was as though she were waving off an invasion of poisonous flies.

"Now, now, class!" she exclaimed with a mixture of tense jollity and clear panic. "We'll have none of *that!* Please turn to page seven in your textbook. I'll read the selection aloud to you first, and then we'll discuss it." She held the book high in the palm of one hand; the other was raised like an admonition, an artistic beckoning.

The reading was from Tennyson's "Ulysses." I had never heard it before. As I listened to her beautiful voice, the old magic took hold, and no amount of peer pressure could keep me from thrilling to the first four lines she read:

> *I am a part of all that I have met*
> *Yet all experience is an arch wherethro'*
> *Gleams that untravell'd world, whose margin fades*
> *For ever and for ever when I move.*

But after that, it was difficult even to hear her. Guffaws sprang up here and there throughout the room. Gladys Simpson whispered something behind her hand to the girl beside her and then broke into fits of giggles. Paper airplanes flew. The wits of grade ten offered comments: "Behold the Bard!" "Bliss! Oh, poetic bliss!" "Hancock! Whocock? Hancock! Hurray!" "Don't faint, class! *Don't faint!*"

I was caught in a stranglehold somewhere between shocked embarrassment and a terrible desire for conceal-ment. No other members of the class shared my knowledge of Miss Hancock or my misery. But I knew I could not hide behind that Duo-Tang folder forever.

It was in fact ten days later when Miss Hancock recog-nized me. It could not have been easy to connect the eager skinny fan of grade seven with the cool and careful person

I had become. And she would not have expected to find a friend in that particular classroom. By then, stripped of fifteen years of overblown confidence, she offered her material shyly, hesitantly, certain of rejection, of humiliation. When our eyes met in class, she did not rush up to me to claim alliance or allegiance. Her eyes merely held mine for a moment, slid off, and then periodically slid back. There was a desperate hope in them that I could hardly bear to witness. At the end of the period, I waited until everyone had gone before I walked toward her desk on the way to the corridor. Whatever was going to happen, I wanted to be sure that it would not be witnessed.

When I reached her, she was sitting quietly, hands folded on top of her lesson book. I was reminded of another day, another meeting. The details were blurred; but I knew I had seen this Miss Hancock before. She looked at me evenly and said quietly, simply, "Hello, Charlotte. How nice to see you."

I looked at her hands, the floor, the blackboard, anywhere but at those searching eyes. "Hello, Miss Hancock," I said.

"Still writing metaphors?" she asked with a tentative smile.

"Oh, I dunno," I replied. But I was. Nightly, in the bathtub. And I kept a notebook in which I wrote them all down.

"Your writing showed promise, Charlotte." Her eyes were quiet, pleading. "I hope you won't forget that."

Or anything else, I thought. Oh, Miss Hancock, let me go. Aloud I said, "French is next, and I'm late."

She looked directly into my eyes and held them for a moment. Then she spoke. "Go ahead, Charlotte. Don't let me keep you."

She didn't try to reach me again. She taught, or tried to teach her classes, as though I were not there. Week after week, she entered the room white with tension, and left it defeated. I didn't tell a living soul that I had ever seen her before.

One late afternoon in March of that year, Miss Hancock stepped off the curb in front of the school and was killed instantly by a school bus.

The next day, I was offered this piece of news with that mixture of horror and delight that so often attends the delivery of terrible tidings. When I heard it, I felt as though my chest and throat were constricted by bands of dry ice. During assembly, the principal came forward and delivered a short announcement of the tragedy, peppered with little complimentary phrases: ". . . a teacher of distinction . . ." ". . . a generous colleague . . ." ". . . a tragic end to a promising career . . ." Howard Oliver was sitting beside me; he'd been showing me flattering attention of late. As we got up to disperse for classes, he said, "Poor old Whocock Hancock. Quoting poetry to the angels by now." He was no more surprised than I was when I slapped him full across his handsome face, before I ran down the aisle of the assembly room, up the long corridor of the first floor, down the steps, and out into the parking lot. Shaking with dry, unsatisfying sobs, I hurried home through the back streets of the town and let myself in by the back door.

"What on earth is wrong, Charlotte?" asked my mother when she saw my stricken look, my heaving shoulders. There was real concern in her face.

"Miss Hancock is dead," I whispered.

"Miss who? Charlotte, speak up please."

"Miss Hancock. She teaches—taught—us grade ten English."

"You mean that same brassy creature from grade seven?"

I didn't answer. I was crying out loud, with the abandon of a preschooler or someone who is under the influence of drugs.

"Charlotte, do please blow your nose and try to get hold of yourself. I can't for the life of me see why you're so upset. You never even told us she was your teacher this year."

I was rocking back and forth on the kitchen chair, arms grasping each other. My mother stood there erect, invulnerable. It crossed my mind that no grade ten class would throw paper airplanes in any group that *she* chose to teach.

"Well, then," she said, "why or how did she die?"

I heard myself shriek, "I killed her! I killed her!"

Halting, gasping, I told her all of it. I described her discipline problems, the cruelty of the students, my own blatant betrayal.

"For goodness' sake, Charlotte," said my mother, quiet but clearly irritated, "don't lose perspective. She couldn't keep order, and she had only herself to blame." That phrase sounded familiar to me. "A woman like that can't survive for five minutes in the high schools of today. There was nothing you could have done."

I was silent. *I could have said something.* Like thank you for grade seven. Or yes, I still have fun with The Metaphor. Or once, just once in this entire year, I could have *smiled* at her.

My mother was speaking again. "There's a great deal of ice. It would be very easy to slip under a school bus. And she didn't strike me as the sort of person who would exercise any kind of sensible caution."

"Oh, dear God," I was whispering, "I wish she hadn't chosen a *school bus.*"

I cried some more that day and excused myself from supper. I heard my father say, "I think I'll just go up and see if I can help." But my mother said, "Leave her alone, Arthur. She's sixteen years old. It's time she learned how to cope. She's acting like a hysterical child." My father did not appear. Betrayal, I thought, runs in the family.

The next day I stayed home from school. I kept having periods of uncontrollable weeping, and even my mother couldn't send me off in that condition. Once again I repeated to her, to my father, "I killed her. We all killed her. But especially me."

"Charlotte."

Oh, I knew that voice, that tone. So calm, so quiet, so able to silence me with one word. I stopped crying and curled up in a tight ball on the sofa.

"Charlotte. I know you will agree with what I'm going to say to you. There is no need to speak so extravagantly. A sure and perfect control is what separates the civilized from the uncivilized." She inspected her fingernails, pushing down the quick of her middle finger with her thumb. "If you would examine this whole perfectly natural situation with a modicum of rationality, you would see that she got exactly what she deserved."

I stared at her.

"Charlotte," she continued, "I'll have to ask you to stop this nonsense. You're disturbing the even tenor of our home."

I said nothing. With a sure and perfect control, I uncoiled myself from my position on the sofa. I stood up and left the living room.

Upstairs in my bedroom I sat down before my desk. I took my pen out of the drawer and opened my notebook. Extravagantly, without a modicum of rationality, I began to write.

"Miss Hancock was a birthday cake," I wrote. "This cake was frosted by someone unschooled in the art of cake decoration. It was adorned with a profusion of white roses and lime green leaves, which drooped and dribbled at the edges where the pastry tube had slipped. The frosting was of an intense peppermint flavour, too sweet, too strong. Inside, the cake had two layers—chocolate and vanilla. The chocolate was rich and soft and very delicious. No one who stopped to taste it could have failed to enjoy it. The vanilla was subtle and delicate; only those thoroughly familiar with cakes, only those with great sensitivity of taste, could have perceived its true fine flavour. Because it was a birthday cake, it was filled with party favours. If you stayed long enough at the party, you could amass quite a large collection of these treasures. If you kept them for many years, they would amaze you by turning into pure gold. Most children would have been delighted by this cake. Most grown-ups would have thrown it away after one brief glance at the frosting.

"I wish that the party wasn't over."